ECHOES OF FIRE

DRAKARN MATES
BOOK 2

KATE RUDOLPH

PROLOGUE

Rath

The burning in my chest felt like I'd swallowed a piece of the lava that runs through this cursed planet. It wasn't the ache of a battle wound, or the sharp stab of betrayal. No, this was different. Fucked up, even by my standards. It clawed, not at my flesh, but at the very core of me, a hollow ache that echoed, a desperate need that whispered, *her*.

I could still taste the subtle sweetness in the air, faint but undeniable. The scent I had caught in the battle against those damned *kervash*, now tinged with something else ... *hers*.

It wasn't just a scent. It was an invasion that was tearing through my carefully constructed wall of control. My internal fires seemed to burn hotter, threatening to set my ruby scales ablaze. I had left, stomped through protocol, and practically begged information from healers like a hatchling but got nothing. Then I'd snarled and still got nothing, but she was there. I *knew* it.

My claws scraped against the stone walls as I pushed open the oversized door of the healer's cavern. It was always too bright in there, the heat crystals pulsating with an irritating light that made my scales itch. The scent of crushed herbs and scented oils filled my nostrils, sickly sweet, it was layered with something else, *her* scent that I had tracked through the air, no matter how faint.

My wings twitched with an energy I couldn't place—part anticipation, part rage at the waiting.

"Rath!" The sharp voice of the head healer, Mysha, cut through the thick air. Her gold scales twitched as she turned, her slit pupils narrowed in annoyance. She was old, ancient even, her voice edged with an authority that only age and skill could grant. Most of my warriors flinched under her gaze.

Even I felt a prickle of unease.

"What in the twin suns do you think you're doing? This is a place of healing, not the war council." Her tone was clipped, practical. She never failed to remind me I was a walking, breathing inferno.

"I need to see the humans." My tone was a low rumble in my chest. My need to get closer to *her* burned so hot that I only managed to maintain a modicum of civility.

She huffed like pressurized steam venting. "For what purpose? They are all various levels of heat sick and need to recover."

"It's important. Council business." I was on the Blade Council. It was *my* business. A technical truth, but the words felt like lies. "One of them had purple in her hair."

Mysha's head tilted back, amusement flickered inside her dark eyes, as though I had just told a rather poor joke. "They are half-dead from the heat and covered in enough dust and sand to choke a *dranith*." She gestured with a clawed hand towards the rows of beds carved into the rock walls, each occupied by a listless human. "None of them is in any shape to speak to the council. They are being medically contained."

My claws curled into fists, sharp points pricking my palms. I wanted to roar my frustration, to demand she bring *her* forth now. But I held back.

Mysha's dismissal stoked the fires in my chest, not that she would care. "I shall decide whether she can speak."

"You will not. Leave, go back to the training grounds and work your rage out." Her voice was firm. "You disturb the healing." She waved her hand as if swatting away an insect.

I fought to contain the roaring in my ears. My wings pushed against the confines of the cavern wall behind me, restless, itching for flight. It was there, faint but unmistakable. Mixed with the sickly herbs and oils, I caught a trace, her aroma. Like a desert flower, sweet, delicate, but with a hint of something wild underneath ... *mine.*

It twisted inside me, an undeniable, visceral pull. It clawed at my throat and settled in my stomach, painful and enticing, the promise of something more.

I took a step toward the beds, my gaze sweeping over figures hidden under white sheets and only the occasional limb visible, looking for a specific face and scent combination. The scent grew stronger as I moved closer.

I wanted to touch, to inhale, to press my nose to her skin and confirm what my body told me was true. My fangs tingled, a sensation that ignited a deeper fire inside me, an ancient urge I'd never truly expected to feel.

"Leave this place, Fire Heart," Mysha's yellow eyes could see my intentions, piercing through my attempts at discretion with a knowing sharpness that bordered on irritation. "I will not let you disturb these patients."

I balled my fist, claws digging into my palm. "You cannot deny me this, elder; I have a *right*." The words hissed past my teeth.

"Your right ends where your tantrums begin." She glared with a look that could burn an entire forest. "If you continue this nonsense, I will summon the guards to escort you out. Consider yourself warned."

I knew from her tone the threat wasn't idle. Mysha would make good on her word. And I still couldn't see *her*. I took a deep breath. It was not worth an all-out battle. I had to be smart. Patient. My mate was there. If the bond was true, then she was more important than anything. "Fine," I ground out, "but I'll be back." Leaving the healing cavern was harder than abandoning an injured soldier on the battlefield.

Once outside, I finally felt the flames inside me simmering down. I needed to think. The sky was ablaze, Volcaryth's suns a painful reminder of the heat that had nearly killed *her*. I couldn't stand the thought of that happening again.

Mate.

The word echoed in my mind. This wasn't some fleeting desire. This was a bond, a connection that defied logic and tradition. My heart thumped in my chest as I let the weight of the situation settle upon me.

A human ... How could I possibly ...

Doubt twisted around my heart, a snake trying to kill my future. What if the connection was false? What if she found me repulsive? What if she didn't want me? Despite all my rage and power, the thought made me flinch.

I was Rath Flame Heart. I commanded legions, I had faced down the greatest warriors and beasts of our time, I was the fire in our clan, yet the possibility of her rejection was more terrifying than anything. The uncertainty made me want to roar, to shake the world until reality shifted.

I looked out over the horizon, at the lights of the suns that shone like two burning eyes, watching me. She would be mine.

I pushed past the fear, the self-doubt, the uncertainty. My wings snapped open, and I took to the sky, ready and determined. The ground rushed away under me as my muscles worked, propelling me upward. A plan was forming.

I needed to see her, to touch her, to mark her as mine. And nothing—especially not a stubborn old healer—would stop me. My roar echoed through the air; a promise written in flames.

ONE
ORLA

The walls breathed.

I pressed my palm flat against the warm stone of one of Scalvaris's cavernous corridors, feeling the faint vibration beneath my fingertips—a rhythmic hum, like the planet itself was pulsing. The rock walls arched above me, their surfaces etched with glowing crystal inlays that spiraled in fractal patterns. My eyes traced the designs, recognizing the deliberate engineering: the veins of heat-resistant mineral branching like capillaries, channeling thermal energy away from inhabited spaces.

Brilliant. A passive cooling system.

"You're doing that thing again," Selene's voice echoed slightly in the vastness around us.

I blinked, lowering my hand. "What thing?"

"The *I'm-about-to-dissect-a-moonrock* stare." She adjusted the strap of the medical kit she had slung over one shoulder, her dark eyes sharp. "You forget to breathe when you're geeking out."

"I'm breathing." I tapped the journal tucked under my arm, its pages already crammed with sketches of the Drakarn's metallic-bark trees—their root systems siphoning groundwater from aquifers even deeper than this underground city. "This isn't just architecture, Selene. It's a *biome.* They've integrated their ecosystem into every structural choice. The heat redistribution alone—"

"Isn't going to matter if you collapse from dehydration." She thrust a canteen into my hands. "Drink. I don't want you falling to heat sickness again."

I grimaced but obeyed, the lukewarm water bitter with electrolyte tablets. Two weeks in that cave after the crash had left all of us humans frayed, but my body still hadn't forgiven me for sprinting through 120-degree winds during our subsequent capture.

The scar along my ribs throbbed faintly as I moved, a reminder of giant claws. It had been nearly a month since I was released from the medical caverns, but my body was still recovering.

Selene watched me swallow, her medic's gaze dissecting every micro-expression. "You're favoring your left side."

"It's a *habit*, not a limp. The muscle's healed." Mostly. I pivoted to distract her, gesturing toward a nearby archway where Drakarn artisans welded alloy into the stone. "Look at those joints—we don't have anything like that back home. The thermal expansion coefficient must be *exactly* matched to the surrounding rock." My fingers itched to take a sample.

She sighed, knowing she couldn't win this. "Just ... don't vanish into another magma vent. Terra'll skin me if I lose you."

"Noted." I smirked, scribbling a hypothesis about the crystal inlays' refractive index. "But if I *do* fall into a lava tube, prioritize saving the journal. It's got a month of soil pH readings."

Selene rolled her eyes but lingered as I crouched to examine a fissure in the floor. Thin tendrils of steam curled upward, carrying a mineral tang that made my sinuses burn. My thumb brushed the tattoo on my wrist—a DNA helix entwined with oak leaves, inked the day I'd defended my thesis.

Adapt or die, my mother's voice whispered in memory. *Life persists where logic says it shouldn't.*

The Drakarn had taken that mantra to staggering heights. Above us, massive roots from the surface trees plunged through the cavern ceiling, their metallic sheen shimmering under bioluminescent fungi. I sketched frantically, labeling the symbiotic relationship: *Fungal networks neutralize soil toxins; roots stabilize subterranean chambers. Mutualism evolved under extreme pressure.*

"Orla." Selene's tone shifted, the playful edge replaced by steel. "You're swaying."

"I'm *balancing*." The lie tasted stale. My vision blurred at the edges as I straightened, the cavern tilting like a ship in a storm.

Her palm gripped my elbow to steady me. "You need rest. Actual rest, not ... whatever this is."

I pulled away gently, nodding toward a distant bridge fortress. Its obsidian spans glittered with embedded heat crystals, their prismatic light fracturing into rainbows across the river below. "I need to *understand*. How they've sustained a civilization here—it's everything I've studied. Everything I ..." *Wanted to prove I could achieve.*

Her gaze softened. "You can't unlock the secrets to the planet in a single day. Maybe one of us could help?"

The words prickled. I adjusted my grip on the

journal, its leather cover worn smooth from years of use. "I work better alone. You know that."

A beat passed. Selene's jaw tightened, but she nodded. "Fine. But if you're not back by nightfall, I'm sending Kira with a tracking beacon. And she'll bring the handcuffs."

I saluted half-heartedly, already turning toward a shadowed tunnel where the walls pulsed with unfamiliar glyphs. "Tell her to bring the scanner on my table. I'll want spectrographic readings."

Her exasperated groan faded behind me as I slipped into the gloom, my boots crunching over gravel that shimmered with flecks of pyrite. The air grew cooler, drier—*climate zones segmented by airflow*, my mind catalogued. A low, resonant chanting vibrated through the stone, harmonizing with the distant rush of the underground river.

I paused, pressing my palm to the wall again. The vibrations sharpened, resolving into a melody that raised the hair on my neck.

Somewhere ahead, the Drakarn were *singing*.

My bruised ribs protested as I quickened my pace, but I ignored them. The scientists who'd laughed at my proposals for Martian biodomes hadn't understood this thirst either—the need to *see*, to map the uncharted edges where theory bled into wonder.

Volcaryth's secrets tempted every part of me, and I'd unravel them one layer at a time.

The chanting thickened like honey, each harmonic layering until the air seemed to vibrate with intent. I followed the sound through a narrowing passage, my boots scuffing against stone worn smooth by centuries of footsteps.

The fungi there glowed cobalt instead of orange, their light catching on glyphs carved into the walls—angular, urgent slashes that my translator couldn't parse. With my subdermal translator I could understand spoken text, but I'd have to learn to read their language the old-fashioned way.

I paused to sketch them, noting how the symbols clustered near ventilation shafts. A prayer? Warning markers? My pencil hovered.

Unknown semantic function. Further study required.

A gust of superheated air rushed from an overhead shaft, carrying the acrid tang of sulfur and something sweeter—burnt amber resin, maybe. My fading purple braid stuck to the sweat-dampened collar of my shirt as I climbed a spiral ramp, each step sending dull fire through my healing ribs. *Idiot. Should've taken Selene's painkillers.* But pharmaceuticals fogged observation, and I needed every synapse sharp.

The ramp ended at a wall about ten feet high. I didn't see a door or any of the chanting Drakarn. At this point, a normal person would have turned away, or maybe just stood to listen.

They didn't have my drive.

Or my climbing skills.

It was one of those things I'd done for fun back on Earth, the precision and risk focusing my mind until all that mattered was the next handhold, the next summit. And ten feet? That was nothing.

I was halfway up the wall before I wondered if this was, *perhaps*, not the smartest move. My side protested every stretch, and my vision was a bit hazy around the edges again. I wouldn't say no to Selene's canteen, but she'd taken it with her.

Maybe the wall was there for a reason.

But I was already halfway up, and the chanting was growing more intense. I just wanted a peek.

The wall ended in a broad walkway that looked out over an amphitheater full of Drakarn. My eyes had to adjust to the eerie twilight. Below me stretched terraces, concentric rings descending toward a central dais where obsidian monoliths speared upward like shattered teeth.

Dozens of Drakarn knelt between them, their winged backs rippling in unison as the chant reached its peak. My breath caught.

I crouched behind a pillar, journal open to a fresh page. The warriors' tails flicked as they moved, their wing membranes taut with precision. Two figures emerged from the shadows—a male with onyx scales threaded with gold, a female who wore a beaded crimson headdress that trembled with each step. They circled the dais, claws scraping grooves into stone already scarred by generations.

Not combat. Too synchronized.

The female lashed her tail, the tip whistling centimeters from the male's throat. He pivoted, wings flaring to buffet her with heated air.

The female reared back, her throat pulsing as she unleashed a roar that made my molars ache. The male responded by dragging his claws through a trough of black sand, sending up a plume that swirled into patterns. Symbols. The same glyphs from the tunnel walls.

My translator implant buzzed uselessly against my skull as the crowd's chanting shifted in tone, their voices splintering into dissonant harmonies that prickled my skin.

A warm trickle slid from my nose. I swiped at it absently, fingers coming away smeared with crimson. *Damn dry air.* The blood droplet hit the stone with a soft *tick.*

Every Drakarn head snapped toward my hiding place.

For three excruciating heartbeats, the cavern held its breath.

Then two hundred pairs of vertical pupils contracted as one, their sulfur-yellow and orange irises fixing on my hiding place. The chanting died mid-syllable, leaving a silence so complete I heard the creak of leathery wing membranes adjusting.

The female's wings fanned into a jagged corona, her snarl revealing twin rows of fangs. The monoliths behind her began to thrum, their surfaces bleeding veins of crimson light that pulsed in time with my rabbit-quick pulse.

Wrong. This is all wrong.

The onyx-scaled male moved first. His wings snapped open with a crack like splitting stone, the gold filaments in his membranes catching the monoliths' hellish glow. Claws longer than hunting knives scored the rock as he ascended the terraces in liquid surges, each lunge closing twenty feet. The air around him shimmered like a living mirage.

"Wait—" My voice was strangled, drowned by the sudden dissonant hissing. A dozen warriors flanked him, tails lashing. Their collective heat hit me in a wave, parching my throat, searing my already sweat-slicked skin.

The female priestess barked a guttural command. My translator spat static, then a mangled phrase: "... *profane ... she defiles the sacrament ...*"

Think. Breathe.

My heel found empty air as I reeled back—the ledge of the wall behind me. Journal pages fluttered as I windmilled my arms, pain screaming through my ribs. The male's talons missed my shoulder by millimeters, shredding my sleeve.

"Please!" I rasped, fingers scrabbling at a fissure in the rock. "I didn't mean—"

A chorus of shrieks answered. Warriors fanned out along the upper ledges, tails coiling to strike. The priestess mounted the dais, her claws raised high. In them glinted a curved blade forged from the same devilish light as the monoliths—a weapon that hurt to look at, its edge warping the air with the threat of pain.

Move. Now. Run.

I lunged for a narrow cleft in the cavern wall—too slow. A spiked tail wrapped my ankle, yanking me onto my back. The impact knocked the breath from my lungs, my vision blurring as scaled hands pinned my wrists. Hot drool splattered my cheek, the male's sulfur-tinged breath scalding my face as he snarled words my translator finally deciphered:

"The defiler must die."

Somewhere in the roaring dark, my mother's voice whispered: *Adapt.*

I twisted my wrist, jabbing a rock sample pick hidden in my sleeve. The male howled as the tungsten spike found the soft junction between his thumb scales. His grip faltered—just enough to roll sideways as the priestess's strike fell.

The sacred blade shattered the stone where my heart had been.

Warriors descended in a storm of claws and blades. I scrambled like a crab over the uneven stone, side screaming in agony, lungs burning with every gasp.

There.

A ventilation shaft—narrow, glowing faintly with the same cobalt fungi from the tunnels. I dove head-first for the claustrophobic passage as another tail yanked at my heels.

"After the defiler!" The priestess's cry chased me as I tried to scramble into darkness. "Let the magma cleanse her sacrilege!"

The shaft walls closed around me, sharp mineral edges tearing skin as I crawled toward faint distant light. Behind, the scrape of claws on stone multiplied.

They were faster.

They were everywhere.

They were *hungry*.

"Wait—I can explain—" My voice drowned in the ruckus.

A clawed hand locked around my bicep, talons piercing fabric and skin. I cried out, journal slipping from my grasp as the male yanked me forward. His breath seared my face, smelling of charred meat and bitter spice. The female stalked closer, her headdress clicking as she spat a word I didn't need my translator to define.

"Execution."

TWO
RATH

The *dranith's* severed claw still smoked in my grip, its jagged edge glowing faintly with residual venom. Knees deep in the ash-choked moat of Scalvaris's eastern gate, I sucked in air thick with the stench of scorched scales and sulfur.

Battle-lust burned through my veins like ore, my scales slick with blood that hissed where it dripped onto smoldering stone. My warriors-in-training panted behind me, their labored breaths echoing the distant wail of steam geysers. The raid had been messy, desperate—dranith weren't usually this bold. It should've made me cautious.

It didn't.

I crushed the claw to powder. "Double patrols on the lava trenches," I growled at Voskath, my voice raw from inhaling cinders. The younger warrior's green scales were dulled by soot, his blade notched from parrying serrated pincers. "The next swarm that tries crawling up our walls, burn their wings off before they—"

Her.

The scent punched through the stink of charred flesh and sulfur—sweet, sharp, *human.* Ozone and damp stone, ink and something floral, cutting through the haze like a blade through smoke. My nostrils flared. My cock stirred.

Fuck.

I spun, wings snapping open with a crack that sent ash devils swirling. The crowded plaza blurred —artisans hauling cracked shields toward the forges, healers hurrying past with stretchers dripping blood, younglings darting between legs to scavenge discarded arrowheads.

No purple-haired human. No delicate throat to mark. But the scent lingered, tendrils of it coiling around me, whispering promises that made my fire churn.

"Rath?" Voskath's blade hovered near my arm, its edge still steaming from dranith blood. "Your eyes are doing the ... flame thing."

I clawed a boulder, relishing the crack of stone.

Sparks skittered across my knuckles. "Tend your patrols."

The temple bell tolled—three jagged peals that meant sacrilege. My pulse roared louder than the geyser fields.

Move. Find. Protect.

I lunged toward the sound, boots crushing discarded weaponry into the ashen soil. The scent thickened near the forge district, where smoke coiled from the chimneys in lazy spirals. My blood boiled hotter with every step. Scales along my ribs flushed crimson—a mating flush, the kind hatchlings giggled about in training caves. Pathetic. Weak.

Unbecoming of a council warrior.

A scream tore through the acrid air. Female. *Hers.*

I was sprinting before the echo died, shoving Drakarn aside. A youngling carrying ore baskets went sprawling, black crystals scattering across the stones. An elder cursed my lineage, her graveled voice lost in the thunder of my pulse. I didn't care. The forge's heat slapped my face as I rounded the final corner and launched, wings pumping as I vaulted the wall surrounding the Forge Temple and landed into ...

Chaos.

Warriors formed a snarling ring around the central dais, their tails lashing in unison like a nest of vipers. Karyseth's priestess cadre chanted, their claws dripping blackened oil into the sacred flame pit. The air reeked of burnt myrrh and something fouler—congealed rage. And in the center ...

Orla.

Two warriors dragged her forward by her absurdly fragile arms, her boots carving furrows through the ash. Blood streaked her temple, matting that violet braid she never tied properly. The frayed ends glinted with tiny metal clasps.

Her shirt hung torn at the shoulder, revealing a lattice of old scars. These *kervash* had dared to touch her.

I would end them all.

Karyseth loomed over the flame pit. "Defiler of the Forge!" The High Priestess's voice slithered through my marrow, colder than the void between stars. "You trespass where fire births honor! You steal sacred sight with ... *this.*"

She held up Orla's journal, pages fluttering like a wounded bird. My mate's—*no, not mate, never claimed*—lips moved silently, calculating something only her clever human mind could fathom. Always thinking, even in the jaws of death.

The priestess hurled the journal into the flames.

Orla jerked against her captors, muscles straining. "Wait! Those were just—"

Karyseth backhanded her.

The crack of flesh on flesh snapped my last thread.

Heat surged through my veins, primal and possessive. My vision tinted red, flames licking at the edges of my sight. The warriors nearest me stumbled back, clutching scaled faces as if seared by my aura. Good. Let them burn.

"Enough."

The word rolled out as a growl, low enough to make the stone underfoot tremble. The crowd stilled. Even the sacred flames bent toward me, the light warping around my smoldering form.

Karyseth's pupils narrowed to dagger points. "Warrior Rath. This doesn't concern the Blade Council."

Orla's gaze locked with mine. Blood welled along her split lip, a crimson bead trembling at the edge before falling. Her pulse rabbited at her throat, a fragile, rapid beat that called to the fire in my blood.

Mine to guard. Mine to claim.

I stepped into the circle.

"It does now."

The priestess's claws gleamed wet with Orla's blood. I counted three drops hitting the dais before my vision cleared enough to see details—the way my mate's left wrist bent at a wrong angle, the charred edge of her journal's cover peeking from beneath Karyseth's scaled foot. My fire surged hotter.

"This *human* scribbled our sacred glyphs," Karyseth hissed, grinding the journal deeper into ash. The stench of burning parchment mixed with Orla's coppery blood. "Stole secrets from the Forge Master's own sanctum. The penalty is—"

"Death by molten ore," the crowd chanted, tails thumping stone in rhythm. Always eager for blood, these zealots. The less faithful Drakarn were smart enough to stay away. But the humans? They were too new here to know better.

Orla coughed, shoulders shaking. Not from fear —from rage. I knew that tremor. Had felt it in my own bones when Ignarath butchers took my sister. Her voice rasped raw but precise. "How could I?" She lifted her chin, blood smearing across that delicate human throat. "This is ridiculous."

Laughter rippled through the warriors, harsh and guttural. Karyseth's tail lashed, sending a burning brazier crashing to the stones. Embers skittered toward Orla's boots. "The Defiler speaks nonsense!"

I stepped closer. Heat radiated off me in visible waves now, making the nearest Drakarn stumble back. My focus narrowed to vital points—the warrior on Orla's left, Krazath, had a weak grip, his thumb joint still swollen from last week's sparring session. The one on her right favored his scarred leg, the old wound from the siege of Ignarath.

It would take nothing to end them now.

Then she looked at me.

Fuck.

Her pupils swallowed the irises—pain or terror, maybe both. But beneath the split lip and bruising, her gaze burned with the same stubborn fire that had let her remain standing after her starbound vehicle crashed on the fiery desert and all that came after that. My claws flexed. She'd nearly died. Would've, if I hadn't—

No. Not now.

Karyseth's scowled. "This is our right, warrior. Leave it."

The crowd parted as Darrokar emerged from the smoke, his human mate, Terra, a shadow at his side. The warlord's obsidian scales glinted with cooling battle filth, his expression unreadable. News must have traveled fast for him to be here already. Farther back in the crowd, I spotted other council members,

Mektar and Zarvash. I didn't know if they'd followed the rumors or if they'd been there for the start of the ceremony.

Orla had no position, no hope of making these zealots see sense. Darrokar could claim her as a concubine, but he was so newly mated and devoted to his human that all would see past the ruse and challenge the claim here and now.

And, having seen his mate's fire, I feared she might strip off his scales one by one for trying.

I met his gaze, trying to come up with some kind of plan that would save Orla. I could only think of one thing. It was all I had thought of for the past month, waiting for the moment to be perfect.

And this moment was as far from perfect as it got.

His fist clenched—once, twice—the old signal. *Proceed. But it'll be your mess to clean up.*

Karyseth caught the gesture. Her snarl revealed cracked fangs. "The human dies. By law. By fire."

Orla's breath hitched. A sound like glass shattering in my ribs.

I moved.

My wing buffeted the left warrior into the flame pit, his scream cut short as he scrambled to safety. My tail snapped the right one's knee before he could react, the wet crunch drowned by the crowd's collective hiss. Orla collapsed forward, and I caught her against my chest, her body shockingly cold against my burning scales.

"*She is mine!*"

My roar shook the cavern. Cracks splintered up the sanctum walls, dust raining from the ceiling.

The words seared my throat, hotter than any battle cry.

Karyseth recoiled, her robes billowing at the hem. The crowd's snarls died mid-breath. Even Darrokar went statue-still, his wingtip twitching once before stilling.

Fuck tradition. Fuck the laws.

Orla trembled against me, her heartbeat thrumming against my scales like a caged songbird. I tightened my grip, claws careful not to pierce her soft flesh.

Mine to shield. Mine to claim.

The truth of it scorched through my veins, leaving no room for doubt.

Orla's bloodied lip beckoned like a flame. My tongue throbbed. Fangs ached with phantom pressure—not a battle-urge, but the need to bite, to brand. My claws flexed against her ribs, the points burning where they dented her shirt's already torn fabric.

Her scent coiled tighter around me with each ragged breath she took—ozone sharpening to lightning-struck stone, floral notes blooming into midnight orchids that only grew in sacred burial caves. My nostrils flared. The priestess's rancid myrrh couldn't mask it now. Couldn't drown what my blood recognized.

"Lies!" Karyseth shrieked again, spittle flying. Her claws slashed the air, etching sigils that made her supplicants recoil. "I see no bond-mark! There has been no vow! This is blasphemy!"

The crowd rippled, warriors hissing, tails lashing. I felt the moment the balance tipped—zealots reaching for blades, acolytes edging closer with hooked chains.

Now.

I flung my wings wide, the membranes casting crimson shadows across the dais. Heat rolled off me in visible waves, warping the air. "You question my honor, Priestess?" my voice boomed, rattling loose stones. "You dare deny the bond?"

The ancient word silenced them. Even Karyseth froze.

Orla's breath hitched. "What's—?"

I unsheathed the heat-crystal dagger at my belt—ceremonial, rarely used, its edge dull but the hilt carved with my clan's fire runes. The blade glowed faintly, responding to my touch.

Hold steady, human.

"Kneel," I commanded, voice steel-edged.

Orla's knees buckled—part shock, part my tail's gentle press behind her knees to make sure she did it. I dropped with her, wings mantling around us both. The dagger's hilt pressed into her palm, her fingers ice-cold against mine.

"Grip it," I growled low so only she could hear. "Tighter. They need to see."

She obeyed, knuckles whitening even as her hand trembled. Good. Smart.

Karyseth lunged forward. "This farce insults the Forge!"

I ignored her, leaning close until my fangs grazed Orla's ear. Her scent flooded me—fear-sweat and ink, sharpening my focus. "When I let go," I murmured, "you put this blade to my throat, *shyrarva.* Understand?"

Her eyes widened, but she nodded. Brave little human.

I released the dagger and threw my head back, baring my throat. My vow shook the sanctum. "By flame and claw, I claim her!"

Orla's arm trembled as she pressed the blade's

edge to my pulse. The crowd gasped. Even Darrokar leaned forward, wings half-spread.

Karyseth's tail lashed. "A trick! The human doesn't know our ways!"

"She holds my fire," I snarled. The dagger's glow intensified, reacting to Orla's touch—my soul recognizing her. The sacred crystals embedded in the hilt ignited, casting her face in a golden glow.

The crowd murmured, claws pulling back.

Almost.

The priestess's claws scraped stone as she stepped closer. "Fire cannot lie," she sneered. "Let the human speak the vow. Let her blood mingle with yours in the sacred flame. Then we'll see this ... *bond.*"

My flames dimmed. *Fuck.* The full ritual required marks, blood, fire—things that would break her. I'd seen initiates scream during bonding ceremonies, and they were Drakarn. No one but the zealots performed the ritual or did something insane like subject themselves to a mating challenge. The gods didn't care, and I would not risk my mate.

Orla was still holding the blade to my throat. Her whisper barely reached me. "What do I—?"

"Silence!" Karyseth's tail cracked.

The dagger trembled in Orla's grip. Her wide

eyes reflected my smoldering scales. So fragile. So mortal. One wrong move, and they'd scorch her to bone.

No.

Instinct surged—fangs aching to pierce, claws itching to claim. My tongue dragged across sharp teeth, tasting the ghost of her blood from when I'd carried her half-dead from the sands a month ago. Sweet. Addictive.

Too much.

I gripped her waist, scales hissing against her shirt's synthetic fabric. Her breath hitched, and she pulled the knife back. Every instinct roared to bite, to brand, to make my claim the truth. But her fragile neck ...

"Trust me," I growled low, the words more plea than command.

Her nod was barely perceptible.

I struck.

My tongue dragged up the salt-damp hollow beneath her ear, every ridge and tastebud igniting as her scent exploded across my senses. Her pulse beat against the flat of my tongue—wild, human-quick, a rhythm that made my cock throb against my battle harness.

Fuck, she was soft. Softer than silk, her skin like gold under my slow, possessive stroke.

A whimper escaped her—high, reedy, cut short by clenched teeth. Her hips jerked against my thigh, seeking friction. My scales flared hotter there, granting her the barest hint of warmth.

Let her burn.

"Steady," I rumbled against her jaw, though my own tail lashed uncontrollably, like I was some unblooded warrior. Her hands fisted against my shoulders, tugging the sensitive roots of my scales in a way that sent fire coiling down my spine. I groaned, the sound traveling from my chest to where our bodies pressed together.

Her answering gasp tasted like victory.

I licked lower, following the tendon straining in her neck. Her blood sang here—spiced fear and burgeoning want, a cocktail that made my fangs ache to pierce. My claws flexed into her hips, pricking through fabric as I hauled her harder against me. Her scent deepened, ozone sharpening to storm-air, damp stone blooming with the musk only a roused mate could shed.

"Mine," I snarled into her skin, lapping at the sweat beading along her collarbone. My wings mantled tighter around us, shielding her from their stares as my tail coiled around her ankle. Let them see her flush. Let them smell her arousal.

Let every fool here know this fire was mine alone to stoke.

Her moan when I reached the scar below her ear nearly undid me—husky, unbidden, a sound that made my cock harden even further.

Fire surged lower. The dagger clattered as her grip slackened, her other hand fisting into my battle harness.

Karyseth's roar shattered the moment. "Enough! Your theatrics insult the Forge!"

I whirled, shielding Orla with my wings. Flames licked my vision. "You doubt the scent-bond? Come closer then, Priestess. See what fire I've kindled."

The challenge hung smoking around us.

No Drakarn moved.

Orla's whisper tickled my ear. "Your scales ... they're glowing."

I glanced down. My ribs shone crimson through ash-streaked plating—mating flush in full blaze. *Fuck.*

Darrokar's wingtip brushed my shoulder. "The bond is ... unexpected," he rumbled, "but evident."

His mate stepped up beside him, human eyes

sharp. "She's marked," Terra said smoothly. "By your laws, that's binding."

Karyseth's tail lashed, but warriors began bowing —first Krazath, then others, until only the priestess stood seething.

Orla's fingers flexed against my chest. "Marked?"

I crushed her closer. "Later."

I locked eyes with Karyseth, letting flames lick across my teeth. "Challenge the bond, Priestess. I'll burn this sanctum to ash before she bleeds."

Silence.

Darrokar stepped forward, his own recent mating scar glinting. "Enough. This is done." His gaze cut to me, unreadable. "The council will discuss this further."

The crowd erupted—outrage, awe, the hungry buzz of scandal. Karyseth's shriek pierced the din, but the warriors were already dispersing, casting wary glances at Orla.

At my mate.

I didn't move. Couldn't.

Orla's whisper tickled my jaw. "Your pulse is racing."

"So it is," I breathed. I couldn't look away from her.

Fuck. I'm doomed.

The big hulking alien who claimed me as his mate had his claws on my arm the whole way back to his chambers. I stumbled once before he slowed his pace, silently adjusting for my shorter legs.

We practically crossed all of Scalvaris until we entered a building I'd never seen before and he took me down a winding staircase, the air growing warmer with each step.

Frankly, I'd had enough of unfamiliar buildings for one day, or for a lifetime. Every time I closed my eyes, I imagined those Drakarn, their claws slashing at me as they called for my blood, my life.

I shivered, despite the heat.

My shirt was in tatters, and I could use a month-long soak in a tub, but I needed to know what the hell was going on. "Where—"

"Hush," he said. "Wait."

I bristled, but there were other Drakarn watching us, hungry eyes taking in the scene. Questions had to wait until we were behind closed doors.

And what mighty doors they were.

The stone door sealed behind us with a resonant thud, and suddenly it was just the two of us in a chamber that smelled of smoldering embers and something darker—smoke and aged leather. Rath released my arm like I'd scalded him. I pressed my back against the door, its engraved runes biting into my shoulder blades as I cataloged the room with frantic precision.

The air tasted like licking a battery. I cataloged the chamber's dimensions through shaky breaths—twenty by thirty paces, hexagonal basalt walls striated with bands of volcanic rock. Heat crystals pulsed yellowish light from recessed niches, their fractal patterns mirroring the city's cooling system I'd observed earlier. It felt like a lifetime ago. Had it been more than an hour? A bed platform dominated the far wall, hewn from a single slab of stone and layered with shimmery silks.

Rath moved to an alcove, his tail trailing behind

him. My traitorous eyes tracked the play of firelight across his scaled shoulders—ruby plates shifting from blood-black to fiery crimson with each breath.

"You'll stay here." He tossed a clay pitcher onto the table. Water sloshed, beading instantly on the heated surface. "I do not trust Karyseth to respect my claim."

I pressed harder against the door, its carvings mapping constellations against my spine. "Your claim? What does that make me exactly? A prisoner? A pet?" The words came out sharper than intended. Adrenaline still sang in my veins, mixing dangerously with the tang of his proximity.

I knew what he'd said in the moment, and a desperate need for survival had me following his lead. But now? When there weren't angry Drakarn breathing down my neck? Things didn't feel so clear.

The pitcher's glaze caught the light as it settled—a ceramic so glassy it could've been forged in Volcaryth's core. My fingers twitched with the urge to test its thermal conductivity.

Anything to anchor myself in data instead of this ... this *thing* coiling under my ribs.

Rath's wings flexed. "You are neither prisoner nor pet." He didn't turn as he spoke, claws methodically stripping off his battle harness. Each piece hit the table with a clatter that made my pulse skip. "The claim grants protection." He paused. "It was the only thing I could think to do in the moment."

The laugh scraped my throat. I gestured to the bed's silks—translucent layers in scarlet. "And *that*? Part of the protection package?"

His spine stiffened. Scales along his shoulders flared, revealing the softer, opalescent hide beneath. My traitorous brain noted the biological purpose— perhaps thermoregulation during threatening displays.

Stop it. He's not—

"I did not plan to claim a mate today. I apologize for not making my bed. Sleep where you wish." Rath finally turned, and god, the full force of him nearly buckled my knees.

Firelight sculpted the planes of his chest, catching on piercings that glinted along the ridges of his scales. A silver ring through one nipple. Another through the soft flesh beneath a clavicle plate. Two more in his ears. Where else was he pierced?

My mouth went dust dry. "The silks are heat-regulated," he continued, oblivious to my internal combustion. "The bathing pool recirculates through geothermal filters. Do not touch the weapons."

I forced my gaze to the arsenal lining the far wall

—blades with crystalline cores, their edges shimmering with residual energy. "Charming decor."

"Practical." He stepped closer, and the air thickened with his scent—ember resin and something muskier. My lungs constricted. "The zealots won't challenge my claim openly. Not tonight, but this affront won't go unanswered."

"How was I supposed to—" I cut myself off, edging along the table, putting its bulk between us. You couldn't argue with zealots. I supposed that was true on any planet.

The journal's loss ached like a phantom limb.

"They don't care about mercy." Rath's tail lashed, sending a stool skittering. "They want blood for their burnt god."

"So you just, what, claimed me? Without even knowing my name?" The words cracked.

"I know your name, Orla Mitchell." Rath stood motionless by the weapons wall, his silhouette haloed in crystal-light. Moonlight from a sky tunnel shaft cut across his scales, turning them to liquid mercury. I counted seven blades within his reach, each more lethal than the last.

"Right." My voice was too loud in the hollow space. "So this ... *claim.* It's a loophole in your laws? Why would claiming me do anything?"

He turned slowly. "Death is the penalty for outsiders who witness the sacred rites. The claim binds your life to mine; as my mate you are ... mine. They cannot harm you without challenging me."

"And if we don't ... click?" Me and relationships hadn't exactly gone places back on Earth. I couldn't see how it would work out between me and someone who wasn't even human.

His nostrils flared, the heat-crystals dimming as if the room itself held its breath. "That is not an option. The zealots are patient hunters."

A shiver skated down my spine. I stepped toward the table, like it could act as some sort of shield. "You didn't answer my question. What am I to you now?"

The silence stretched, thick with the creak of leathery wings adjusting.

"A problem," he said at last.

I barked a laugh. "Charming."

"One I will solve." He moved closer, claws still glinting. My pulse stuttered—an autonomic response, I told myself. Nothing more. "You will stay here. Keep out of trouble. When the threat passes ..."

"You'll unclaim me?" My thumb rubbed the DNA helix tattoo on my wrist, the ink gritty with ash. "How convenient." Was I angry about that? Wasn't it what I wanted? I was still shaking with residual fear and couldn't get control of my feelings.

His growl vibrated in my molars. "There is no *unclaiming*. The bond is ... permanent."

The word buzzed between us like a live wire.

I gripped the table's edge. "You didn't think to mention that before tongue-bathing me in front of your entire cult?"

"Would you have preferred the pyre?"

Yes, part of me wanted to snap. The part that still smelled burning journal pages. But the larger part—not the scientist, but the woman—was blisteringly grateful to be saved. And curious.

What did Rath look like under those leathers?

I *did not* look back to the sleeping slab.

Rath stepped closer, each footfall thundering through the volcanic stone. The heat radiating from him intensified, warping the air between us. My traitorous pulse quickened as his shadow engulfed me, the ridges of his scales catching the firelight in fractal patterns that danced across my skin.

"Convenience and survival are often at odds," he rumbled, his voice lower than the geothermal hum in the walls. His claw traced the table's edge beside my hand, black talon scoring a hairline fracture in the stone. "You'll adapt."

"Adaptation requires time. You've given me nothing but vague threats and ..." My gaze flicked to the bed platform, its silks shimmering with invitation. *Damn it.* "Theatrics."

His nostrils flared, the piercings along his brow ridge glinting as he leaned in. "You want data, scientist?" His breath scorched my temple. "Your pulse is elevated. You're sweating. And your scent ..." A low growl rumbled through my shoulder where his claw brushed my tattered sleeve. "Betrays more than your words."

I jerked back, the table's edge biting into my thighs. "It's about a thousand degrees in here."

"Liar." His tail lashed. "You reek of ..." His tongue flickered out, tip grazing my collarbone. My knees almost buckled at the sensation—a thousand nerve endings igniting under that brief contact. "Curiosity."

An echoing knock shattered the charged silence like a stone through glass. Rath's growl vibrated through me once more as he stalked toward the door, his tail lashing a warning pattern against the tiles. I sagged against the table, my fingers trembling as I pressed them to the spot his tongue had touched— skin still buzzing as though he'd branded me with electricity.

He wrenched the door open with a snarl. "This is not—"

Terra stood framed in the archway, her green eyes sharp as broken bottle glass. She didn't flinch at Rath's bared fangs, her gaze sliding past him to lock onto me before she pushed past him and entered the room. "You're alive. Good."

I straightened, tugging my shredded sleeve over the scratch marks on my arm. "Mostly."

Rath tried to further block her path, wings flaring. "Leave."

"I just spent a half hour listening to my mate describe *in detail* what he plans to do to you. Do not test me right now." Terra cocked her hip, hand resting near the plasma pistol at her thigh. "We need to talk."

The standoff crackled—two predators sizing each other up. I edged around the table, hyper aware of Rath's scales flushing crimson along his spine.

"It's fine," I said.

His claws flexed. "She's—"

"My friend. Let her in."

Rath's pupils narrowed to slits, but he stepped aside with a hiss that made the heat crystals dim. Terra strode in, her boots leaving ashen prints on the polished stone.

"Cute love nest," she said, surveying the weapon-lined walls. "Very ... dungeon-core chic."

I choked back a laugh. "He's going for murderous hermit aesthetic."

Rath made a rumbling sound in the back of his throat. "As I said, this mating was unplanned."

I looked over at my ... mate. The word felt strange in my head. "Can we have some privacy?"

He opened his mouth, and I could almost hear the denial. Then he nodded. "Anything for you, *shyrarva*. I shall go see that your things are moved here."

"Don't call me that." But I was speaking to his retreating wings and then the closed door.

That left Terra and I alone.

"So they're all like that," she muttered. "Karyseth's work?" she asked, nodding towards my torn shirt. Her voice stayed neutral, but the set of her jaw betrayed her anger.

"Priestly hospitality." I forced a smile, leaning into the familiar routine of banter—Terra's no-nonsense words, the faint citrus scent of her soap. Grounding. Human.

She clicked her tongue. "I expect Selene will be breaking down that door as soon as she hears. You've still got cracked ribs that never fully healed. And this

—" Her fingers brushed the crescent marks on my wrist where Rath's claws had gripped too tight. "The Drakarn aren't gentle, even when they try. I don't like this."

I stared at the wall of weapons, their edges catching the light in prismatic shards. "It kept me breathing."

"For now." Terra stepped back, her gaze sharp as a scalpel. "It wasn't just Rath that Darrokar was yelling about. This situation with the Forge Temple could get bad. Some on the council are far more sympathetic than they are to us." Her tone softened. "He called you *shyrarva*. That's a mating name; he spent time thinking about it. Whatever's going on with him—"

The alien word prickled my skin like sunburn. "It's just part of the act."

"You think this is an act? Is that what he said?" She launched herself up so she was sitting on Rath's —our?—table.

"You think he's for real?"

There is no unclaiming.

"Drakarn don't fake bond-marks. That tongue thing he did?" She fanned herself exaggeratedly. "Hot damn."

I hated how my cheeks flamed.

Terra's boots swung inches above the floor, the casual motion at odds with the tension in her voice. "The Blade Council tolerates us because Darrokar's mate-bond gives me standing. But Karyseth's faction?" She tapped her fingernails against the table, each click echoing like a gunshot. "They've been itching for an excuse to purge 'weakness' from Scalvaris. You just handed them a flamethrower."

I traced a fracture in the stone, my nail catching on microcrystalline edges. "So the solution is ... what? Let Rath keep pretending we're soulmates?" The word tasted absurd, like trying to swallow a neutron star. "There have to be protocols for cultural misunderstandings. Mediated dialogues—"

"This isn't a UN summit." Terra hopped down, boots scraping against the floor. "This is their holy law. Either the bond's real, or it's heresy. No third option." She gripped my shoulders, her callouses catching on torn fabric. "If the Forge Temple can prove this is a sham? They'll execute you. Then they'll come for the rest of us, arguing humans corrupt their warriors' honor."

"Rath said the claim was permanent. That there's no undoing it."

"Because there isn't." Terra's gaze drifted to the silks pooled on the sleeping slab. "Drakarn bonds aren't human. Darrokar nearly ripped a warrior's throat out for brushing against me during the monsoon feasts." Her eyes raked over the fresh scab on my lip. "When Rath tasted you …"

Heat flooded my cheeks again. "It was nothing."

"Bullshit." She released me to pace past Rath's arsenal, fingers trailing over a curved blade.

The memory of his tongue flicking my collarbone ignited phantom static across my skin. "He called me a problem."

"And stared at you like you're a damned supernova." Terra spun a dagger, the edge catching firelight. "Bond-marks are … physical. Biological. Believe me; I know. The council could demand proof." Her gaze dropped to my neck, where Rath's tongue had left invisible burns. "If they test you—"

"*Test?*" The word curdled in my stomach. I pressed a hand to the scar below my ear, still humming with phantom heat. "What kind of test?"

The door groaned before she could answer. Rath filled the archway, his scales dulled to burnt umber in the low light. A leather satchel hung from his claw, spilling familiar items—my scanner, a bundle of rock samples, the cracked remains of my field goggles. And some clothes. He set it down with surprising care, the contents clinking.

"Your possessions," he rumbled. "Including this." From his belt, he produced my journal—singed but intact, its pages warped from fire.

I lunged forward, snatching it before logic intervened. The leather cover was a bit scorched. "You stole this from the pyre?"

His tail twitched. "Salvaged. Before the final blaze."

The admission startled me. I flipped through crackling pages—sketches of ventilation shafts intact, soil pH tables legible beneath soot stains. My throat tightened. "Thank you."

Rath inclined his head, the gesture almost courtly. "Of course, *shyrarva*."

The alien word pricked like a splinter. "I have a name."

"We'll talk about this more later," Terra said before Rath and I could get into it. "Just stay strong. Sell this bond." She turned toward the door and paused before looking back. "If you need someone to talk this out, you know where I live."

"My mate can speak with me," Rath growled.

Terra and I both rolled our eyes.

"Thanks," I told her. "I'll think about what you said."

As if I could think about anything else.

I NEEDED TO SIT. The adrenaline crash had settled into an ache in my skull. I crossed the room, wanting distance from him, and dropped onto the corner stone bench. The basalt was cold beneath me despite the warmth radiating off the chamber walls.

I gripped the edge of the bench and pressed my palms tight against its rough surface. My mind played the scene from the temple again, unspooling every scream and snarl until I winced. The memory of Karyseth's claws swiping inches from my chest made my pulse race. My body ached from running, from falling, from everything.

"You should take the bed," Rath's voice broke the silence. It carried low and steady, like the rumble of distant magma.

I looked up. He was standing near the platform, his tail coiled tightly behind him, his claws flexing in and out. The lines of his face were rigid—the air of a creature used to commanding obedience—but his tone had softened. "You need rest."

I shook my head, trying for a semblance of control. "I'll make do here."

"You aren't fine." He stepped closer, his broad shoulders tense. The weight of his presence filled the room like a flame creeping closer, heating everything in its path. "You're bruised."

I laughed, bitter and quiet. "Don't worry about me. You've done enough already."

He looked startled at my words, like I'd struck him. His chest expanded with a sharp inhale, faint embers lighting beneath his scales. "Do not mistake necessity for—" He stopped, his tail lashing against the floor. "The claim was to save your life. But it is my responsibility now to see to your health."

"I didn't ask for that."

"No," he admitted, the single word scraped raw. "But you are." He stepped closer still, heat rolling off him in waves. "And I protect what is mine."

The word *mine* sent a shiver through me. I tried to suppress it. Failed. I stood, the aching protests of my body ignored, and faced him—one hand gripping the edge of the bench for steadiness, the other clenched into a fist by my side. "I am not *yours*. I am my own person. And I can take care of myself." Not that I was doing very well at that right now.

If my defiance rattled him, he didn't show it. His slitted pupils narrowed further, the faintest growl vibrating from deep within his chest. "You can barely stand."

I glared at him. "Yeah? Whose fault is that?"

The growl cut off, his jaw tightening as heat flared briefly along his scales. He didn't respond.

I forced myself to break eye contact, grabbing the nearest folded blanket from edge of the sleeping platform. "I'll sleep over here tonight," I said, my voice sharp but quieter now. "I've crashed on a couch before." Of course, those couches had cushions. But the Drakarn were not soft. Apparently, they didn't care about comfort.

"You're being stubborn," he replied.

"And you're being overbearing."

A long pause stretched between us. Eventually, Rath exhaled a sharp breath. It came out like a hiss, his tail flicking the edge of the floor. "Fine." His voice was cold, the diplomacy gone. "Do what you want."

The space between us rippled with tension. I sat heavily on the couch, wrapping the blanket around myself stubbornly. My ribs flared a fresh complaint, but I ignored it.

Rath settled onto the stone platform across the room. His movements weren't loud, but every scrape of claw against obsidian battered my senses. He sat rigidly, his broad back facing me. The glow of the heat crystals cast faint, pulsing patterns over his wings, which drooped slightly now, less tension in the sinewed muscles around them.

We didn't say anything else. I pulled the blanket tightly around my shoulders and propped a pillow between the wall and my aching ribs. My body begged for stillness, but my mind wouldn't quiet.

The events of the day looped through my thoughts like a jagged-edged film reel. Karyseth's accusing snarl, the hissing crowd, the sensation of Rath's claws tearing through the zealots' ranks to claim me—each memory spiraled into the next. My fingers drifted to my neck where his tongue had left an invisible brand, heat still radiating beneath the skin every time I thought of the phrase, *"She is mine."*

I squeezed my eyes closed, trying to focus on the pain—more tangible sensations. My ribs, still tender, resisted when I shifted positions. My palms stung where I'd scraped against jagged rock while fleeing. My shoulders cried out from hours of tension. The couch was too hard to offer relief, no matter how I contorted myself.

Sleep didn't come easily. My mind stayed alert, cataloging every sensation, every flicker of uncertainty crawling over my skin. The warmth of the chamber wrapped around me like a smothering blanket, layering atop the press of Rath's invisible gaze. I doubted he'd turned to look, but I could still feel him

—could hear his steady breaths above the ambient noise of the city. There was something about his proximity that made it impossible for me to relax, no matter what position I shifted into.

My ribs rebelled again, a sharp ache cutting through my chest. I groaned and bit back a curse.

"You're still awake." His voice broke the quiet, startling me.

"I'll sleep eventually."

I didn't.

FOUR
RATH

The River Market roared with life as we entered, its heartbeat pulsing alongside the river winding through the city's core. Reflections from the water and heat crystals played across market stalls and stone ceilings, casting moving shadows.

Voices rose and fell in waves: merchants hawking fire-etched jewelry, farmers shouting over crates of krysfruit, and warriors exchanging boasts while sharpening their lava-forged blades. The heat radiating from the stones beneath our feet pressed upward, intensifying with the crush of bodies.

Orla walked at my side, her eyes darting across the crowd with equal parts curiosity and unease. I let my wing brush against her, and she gave me a wavering smile. My tail flicked once, irritated—not at her, but at the stares and whispers that followed us, and the way her shoulders drew tight under their weight.

Let them stare. Let them see my claim and understand the price of disrespect.

It had been two days since the claiming, since she'd held a blade to my throat, and I'd tasted her pulse under my tongue. Two days of torture where she kept her distance but hadn't left my quarters. Two days of her sleeping in a little burrow against one wall made of scavenged silks and pillows as if I hadn't offered her sole use of the bed.

So close, and yet I was not invited to touch.

Not yet.

She'd wrapped herself in one of my spare tunics, cinching the fabric at her waist with a belt she'd found in her satchel.

My mate. *Mine.*

That truth burned beneath my ribs, stronger than the voices around us.

The problem was obvious. My bond with Orla—a human, an outsider—would be challenged. The priestess had made her doubts clear, and already the rumors were taking hold. This walk wasn't just for her safety.

Scalvaris thrived on appearances. If they saw us

together, if they saw her protected and claimed, perhaps the whispers would quiet—or at least recede to the darkest shadows where they would eventually die.

But her discomfort was a persistent stress against my instincts. It was as real as the storm-salt scent that clung to her. Her pulse stayed steady, not spiked with fear, but the tension in her jaw and the press of her lips said enough.

I reached down and brushed the back of my hand against hers. She blinked, her sharp chin tilting toward me. She drew in a quick breath, and the faint color blooming in her cheeks sparked something in my chest I didn't fully understand.

"Are we here to get something in particular?" she asked, her gaze shifting to a vendor selling polished stone carvings.

"I thought you would like to see the market," I lied.

Her thin brows rose, disbelief plain. I tightened my wings against my back, though their membranes itched to flare in denial. She was clever, my Orla. Too clever.

"This has nothing to do with flexing your wings at everyone here?" Her tone was dry, though a flicker of curiosity lurked behind her words.

"Nothing," I said evenly.

Her snort was quiet but unmistakable. "Sure. I'll play along. Show me the market, which I have definitely not walked through almost every day since I got here."

We passed a group of younglings crouched near a tiled fountain, their eyes darting toward Orla before flicking away. She stiffened at their scrutiny, and I swallowed the growl that threatened to rise. My scales felt hot against the back of my neck, but I forced myself to stay composed.

"Drakarn diplomacy at its finest," Orla muttered, crossing her arms over her chest.

I stopped at a stall displaying stylized carvings made from heat crystals. Orla paused beside me, her eyes narrowing as she studied the goods. I reached for a hand-sized crystal shaped like a flowing wave, its edges pulsing faintly with gold light.

Her brow furrowed. "What are you doing?"

"They call this enlightenment stone," I said, avoiding her question. "It's said to reflect the holder's true emotions."

"We have something like that on Earth," she said, her fingers twitching toward the edge of the table. I knew the habit—her engineer's instincts itching to take things apart, to understand their workings.

"They're called mood rings. They just react to body heat."

The merchant, a gray-scaled artisan with worn claws, grunted. "Pretty. For a pretty lady."

I stiffened at his tone, but Orla only shrugged, her lips tilting in faint humor. "Pretty's not bad."

I placed the crystal in her palm, ignoring the merchant's sharp intake of breath. Drakarn didn't give gifts lightly, not without meaning. But I wanted her to feel something other than the weight of this unfamiliar world.

Her fingers curled around the crystal, her lashes lowering as she examined the glow. I held my breath as she murmured, "Fascinating," the word so soft it barely carried above the noise. The crystal's gold hue deepened to fiery orange where her fingers pressed into its surface.

My tail curled instinctively, satisfaction simmering low in my chest. Just as quickly, her hand hovered, the crystal held out in silent offering to return it. "It's beautiful, but I—"

"Keep it," I said sharply enough that the merchant flinched. "It's yours."

She hesitated, her lips parting in protest. But when her eyes met mine, I saw the shift. Her resistance softened, something unspoken lingering in its place.

"Alright," she said at last, the word carrying no edge.

I felt the tension in my shoulders ease as I handed over a few coins and we moved on.

The market's edge opened into a quieter stretch, where the crowd thinned and the noise faded to scattered conversations. The cobblestones beneath our feet gleamed faintly, their grooves worn smooth by countless years of footsteps. Here, the air didn't press as heavily, though Orla's posture stayed stiff.

"This ..." Her voice broke the silence, hesitant. "All of it. It's a little overwhelming. I feel like everyone's staring at me. Even more than usual."

I fell into step beside her. "It will calm down. I'm sure some warrior will make a spectacle of himself, and all eyes will turn to him."

She let out a short laugh. "Like he'll claim a human in the middle of a crowded temple to save her from certain death?"

I considered her for a moment before speaking. "When you put it like that, I concede it may take a little more time."

"Great."

Dwelling on possibilities would do us no good. "Come," I said finally, gesturing to an alcove ahead. Its sloped ramp curved upward, a decent launch point.

She glanced at the entrance, her lips pressing into a thin line. "Where—"

"Not far. Trust me."

Her brow arched, skepticism plain. "The last time I trusted you ..."

I smiled faintly and held out a hand.

She walked with me. Each step carried us higher, the market noise getting fainter. I glanced back once, checking her footing, but she moved steadily, her gaze focused.

She squinted at the view, her hands braced on her hips. "Is this ... a vent? You really know how to show a girl a good time."

I barked a laugh. "A vent? No, this is a launch point. From here, the air will carry us above the city." My wings flexed slightly. "Would you like to see it?"

Her brows furrowed, her lips parting in what I guessed was an objection. "Wait— You— What are you suggesting?"

I stepped closer, letting my wings spread to catch the air. "Fly with me."

Her gaze darted to the cave ceiling high above, then back to me, her hesitation clear. But there was something else, something fragile that flickered behind her sharp exterior. She was a scientist, a curious woman, and fearless enough to wonder. She bit her lip, and I could see the moment curiosity won out.

She stepped close. "If you drop me, I swear—"

I grinned, something warm unfurling beneath my ribs. "I wouldn't dare."

She stiffened as I wrapped an arm around her waist, my claws brushing the fabric of her tunic to steady her. My tail curled lightly around her knees, ensuring her balance, and she made a surprised sound that went straight through me. I had to clench my jaw as blood rushed to my cock. The warmth of her seeped through the thin layers of clothing, her scent filling the space between us.

"Relax," I murmured when her hands clutched reflexively at my shoulders. Her tension rippled through me, though it was matched by a steady courage I couldn't help but admire. "I have you."

Without giving her time to second-guess, I crouched slightly and leapt, wings snapping open to catch the warm spirals of air. The force of the launch pressed her tighter against me, her gasp muffled as the currents caught us, my wings lifting us effortlessly into the sky.

Below, the ledge and the narrow shaft vanished, swallowed by the shimmering cityscape of Scalvaris. The river wound through the volcanic architecture like glass, its glow constant against the dark stone. The spires of the city stretched high to where they brushed the edges of our cavernous home in some places.

Orla clung to me, her arms locked tightly around my shoulders. Her breath came in quick bursts against my neck, but her fear began to ebb as she tilted her head to take in the view.

"This is," she started, her words faltering. She leaned slightly, her gaze sweeping over the expanse below us. "This is incredible."

I banked slightly, adjusting my wings to glide along the natural updrafts. "The city looks different from above. No busybodies."

"It's ..." Her voice trailed off again, her brow furrowing as if searching for the right words. Finally, she shook her head. "I don't even know how to describe it."

Her reaction stirred something deep in my chest. I couldn't explain why her awe mattered to me, but it did.

Her grip loosened slightly, and the tension in her shoulders melted away as she adjusted to the rhythm of the air. For the first time in days, she looked at peace.

I angled us toward the higher cavers, their jagged entrances almost invisible against all the rock. An even narrower fissure came into view, its entrance obscured by shadows. I guided us inside, the currents shifting as we dipped into the hidden space. The air cooled slightly, the light dimming as we flew through a shaft barely large enough for my wings until the cavern opened up around us, and a large skyshaft illuminated the room around us in natural light.

Luminous heat crystals lined the walls, their glow pulsating in vibrant waves of red, orange, and blue. Pools of water teeming with life shimmered across the cavern floor, their surfaces reflecting the light in rippling patterns.

I landed softly on a ledge near the cavern's center, releasing Orla carefully. Her feet found solid ground, but she didn't move immediately. Her head tilted back as her eyes widened, taking in the light and color that surrounded us.

"This," she said, her voice barely above a whisper. "This is..."

There were no words. I stepped back and let her take it all in.

She turned in a slow circle, her fingers brushing

the stone walls. The light danced across her skin, painting her in shifting hues. "It's like nothing I've ever seen. How is this here? Untouched?"

"This is a sanctuary," I said simply. "Few know of it. I discovered it when I was a boy."

Her gaze flicked to me, questioning. "And you brought me here."

"Yes," I said, my tone steady. "Because I wanted you to see it."

She hesitated, her fingers pausing over a crystal vein that pulsed faintly under her touch. "Why?"

The question hung between us, heavier than I'd expected. I could have given her a hundred reasons—about trust, about showing her my world—but the truth felt too raw, too unformed to articulate. She was my mate. All that I was belonged to her.

"Because you should," I said at last. "This place is ... it's what Scalvaris is beyond the fire and ash. It's what matters."

She studied me for a moment, her expression unreadable. Then she turned back to the crystals, her hand tracing the patterns with a softness I hadn't seen in her before.

"It's beautiful," she murmured.

I didn't respond, letting her take it in. Her presence here felt right in a way I couldn't explain, like the cavern itself welcomed her. Watching her, I felt something settle deep in my chest—something dangerous; something I couldn't yet name.

She moved toward one of the pools, crouching at its edge. The liquid shimmered faintly, its surface undisturbed. Her reflection wavered as she leaned closer, her curiosity pulling her into the moment.

But then, her footing shifted. A loose stone cracked under her weight, and she wobbled, her arms flailing for balance.

I lunged, my wings flaring as my tail wrapped around her waist. She yelped softly as I pulled her back, her feet dangling briefly above the edge before I set her down, steadying her with both hands.

Her chest rose and fell rapidly, her pulse a beat against my palms. "Um ... thanks," she muttered, her cheeks a charming shade of red.

"Be careful," I said, my voice low. My grip on her tightened briefly, the edge creeping in despite myself. "This place isn't forgiving."

She looked up at me, her face inches from mine. Her breath was warm against my jaw, and for a moment, the cavern seemed to shrink around us, the air thick with something unspoken.

"It's just a pool of water," she reconsidered.

"Right? It's not acid or filled with some sort of flesh-eating bacteria, is it?"

"It's water," I confirmed. But I hadn't let her go.

I didn't move, my gaze locked on hers. The urge to close the distance, to claim what was mine, burned through me, sharp and insistent. But I held back, the weight of the moment balanced on a fragile edge.

Her eyes—so green they put the finest gems of Scalvaris to shame—held mine with an intensity that made the cavern feel smaller, the air between us warmer. She was breathing a little faster now, her chest brushing lightly against me with each inhale. The moment was pressing in on her too.

Good. She felt it.

Everything about her drew me in—her stubborn tilt of the chin, the faint smudge of krysfruit still on her cheek from earlier, the way her hair caught the flickering light and haloed her head in fire.

My mate. Everything in me roared with the truth of that word.

I shifted closer, just a fraction. Her gaze dropped to my lips, then shot back to my eyes, a quick flicker that didn't escape me. She was thinking about it. I had to choke back a groan as her tongue darted out, wetting her lips.

Orla, my storm-salt human, had no idea the ruinous effect that small action had on me.

Her lips were full, softly curved, and I imagined how they'd feel against mine—how they'd taste. The memory of her pulse beneath my tongue still haunted me, that intoxicating warmth lingering in my senses long after we'd pulled apart. Giving her a mark, a claim she couldn't ignore, had been the only thing that quelled my lust that night.

For now.

I angled my body closer, allowing my wing to brush against her. Her quiet intake of breath told me she wasn't entirely unaffected. The tension in her shoulders had loosened, her weight shifting ever so slightly toward me.

The cavern echoed around us, the water's soft lap against the stones providing a rhythmic beat. She tilted her head up just a fraction, presenting that delicate curve of her neck, and my mind spun with the images of my teeth grazing her soft flesh, of her moans vibrating through me as I worshipped her body.

Calm down.

Patience.

"I—" she began, her voice barely a whisper, but she didn't continue.

My tail, still possessively curled around her lower body, loosened its grip just enough to let her feel the tension coiled in me. She looked down, surprised by the delicate hold I had, then back at my face, her eyes wide and unguarded.

That thought alone stoked the fire within me. My lips twitched in a half-smile as I imagined her, hair wild and flushed, biting her lip as she hovered over me in our bed. *Ours.*

She caught her lip between her teeth—and there it was again. That small action, that sliver of vulnerability that threatened to rip what little control I had left to shreds. I leaned in just a breath more, my mouth a breath from hers, the heat between us undeniable.

But she stepped back, her hand brushing against her waist where my tail had been. "You're right," she said, her tone lighter now, almost teasing. "I should be more careful."

I exhaled, the tension in my chest easing just enough to speak. "You certainly keep me on edge."

Her lips quirked faintly, the barest hint of a smile. "I'll take that as a compliment."

If I wasn't careful, this human would be the end of me.

FIVE
ORLA

Rath's quarters felt cramped, and not because of the walls. The space itself was more than large enough—ample room for his oversized bed platform, his towering racks of weapons, and his peculiar collection of volcanic relics that sat arranged with obsessive neatness. Even the row of silken tunics in his closet space that I hesitated to touch hung spaced precisely apart.

Despite the size, the air seemed to press in on me, heavy and unrelenting.

I didn't care if the temperature-controlled sheets were some engineering marvel or if Rath thought my scanner and rock samples from my satchel should be displayed like trophies. None of that mattered—not when every surface of the room exuded *him*.

His heat clung to the walls. His scent—the faint aroma of charred air and metal—saturated the space. His essence lingered like those wings of his, wrapping around me even in his absence.

I could only take so much before I went crazy.

Two days after that ... *moment* in the hidden cavern, and I needed an escape.

Rath had left early in the morning, mumbling something about council meetings and an overdue conversation with Darrokar. For someone so usually direct, his reluctance to step away had been blatant.

His gaze had lingered over me, eyes gleaming with an unshakable intensity that seemed to bypass verbal barriers. He'd stopped masking it. That heat, that quiet certainty—it was everywhere now. And it filled the chamber to the brim, a threat ... or a promise.

I pulled one of his tunics tighter around myself, its fabric absurdly light but efficient against the wind in the tunnels. My usual work shirt hadn't seen the light of day since the temple disaster, shredded into something unwearable. I had other clothes I could wear, but if I was being honest—with myself, at least—I liked the way the tunic faintly carried his scent.

Pathetic, Orla.

I slipped out of the room before my thoughts

could spiral deeper. His chambers sat deep enough within Scalvaris that wandering unnoticed wasn't hard—except for the prickling sense that I was doing something wrong.

Whether it was a paranoid trick of the mind or those zealots lurking just out of sight, I didn't know. But it didn't stop me from pressing forward. My boots echoed against the carved stone floor as I threaded through corridors, the veins of heat crystals casting faint orange light along my path.

The carved arteries of the city felt alive, their high-ceilinged passages whispering with the pulse of steam vents and rushing water systems below. Crossing busier intersections felt overwhelming—hissing pipes venting heat, Drakarn warriors sharpening blades, and artisans hauling crates of glimmering crystals. Bits of guttural words reached me in clipped fragments, their consonants rippled with unmistakable curiosity whenever I passed. I kept my head down.

By the time I veered into the quieter halls leading toward the human quarters, I felt brittle. Like one wrong breath would snap me in two.

The enclave for the crew had been carved into an alcove smaller and plainer than any Drakarn living space that I'd seen—not that I'd seen many, but

I welcomed the dimmer atmosphere. The air felt cooler here, soothing the perpetual flush lingering on my skin.

I hesitated near the edge of the communal space, listening. Kira was murmuring to someone, possibly baking if she had the supplies, and Eden's habitual humming—no surprises there. But when I heard Selene's voice—a calm, familiar low timbre edged with her usual combat-medic steadiness—I knew exactly where I was headed.

Knocking softly at her door, I leaned into the cool stone wall.

"Come in," she called easily, warmth coating her voice.

Selene's quarters weren't much bigger than mine had been, yet she'd managed to make the small space her own. Every piece of equipment—medical or otherwise—sat in perfect order on her table. The faint scent of antiseptic mixed with something floral, maybe herbal tea. She glanced up as I stepped inside, a roll of bandages still in her hands, her braid shifting over one shoulder.

"Big, red, and broody let you sneak away?" she teased, setting the bandages down with a flourish.

I snorted, slumping into one of the stiff-backed chairs she'd tucked against the wall. "Not exactly.

He's in a meeting. I got away before he could do anything about it. Talk about suffocating." The words tasted wrong on my tongue. Not quite a lie but definitely not the truth. Rath had been accommodating, kind, without pressing for anything I wasn't ready to give.

Her brows quirked, a wry smile tugging at her lips. "Could've fooled me. Kaiya saw you two in the market. She said it was *quite* the sight."

I groaned, my hands flying to cover my face. "Please. Just don't." My voice was half-laugh, half-groan.

Selene laughed softly, leaning against the table, arms folded. "Sorry, sorry. No teasing. Not right now, at least." She gave me a sympathetic look. "For real, how is it?"

Before I could answer, a familiar figure filled the doorframe briefly, tray in hand, likely on her way to the communal oven. Kira caught neither my gaze nor Selene's, murmured something apologetic, and disappeared down the corridor again before I could even finish my frown.

"Is she okay?" I asked. She'd seemed depressed ever since I woke up there. But maybe that was just how she was; it wasn't like I'd known her before all of *this.*

Selene's sigh was deep and slow. "She's hanging on, but she's not okay. Her sister was on the other side of the ship before the crash. The uncertainty is worse than grief; it's a wound she can't stop picking at."

My stomach twisted, guilt mixing uncomfortably with weariness. "That's terrible," I muttered, staring blankly at the polished surface of the table. It was bad enough knowing I'd never see Earth again, but I'd made that decision when I signed up to leave. Volcaryth wasn't the intended destination, but I was starting to adjust, at least a little. To lose a sister, though?

Selene's voice softened again. "We're all dealing with something," she said, her careful gaze settling on me. "Which brings us back to you and your Drakarn shadow. I want details. How did this happen?"

I hesitated, fumbling for words that didn't all sound hysterical. "I ... have no freaking clue," I finally said, picking absently at one loose thread in my borrowed tunic sleeve. "I'm stuck with him—and part of me, god ... I think part of me might actually ..."

"You're allowed to like him, Orla." Her smile was faintly amused but far from cruel. "No one back on

Earth is going to chastise you for caring about someone. Even fire-breathing aliens."

"They don't breathe fire," I said, as if that was the important part. "I don't even *know* him. And this mating thing? This ... supposed mystical, permanent 'bond'? It feels absurd. We're from different planets. How can there be something ... meant to be?"

She didn't laugh this time. "Terra's figured it out with Darrokar." Her voice held a quiet steadiness, the kind reserved for those who'd already pieced together the advice you weren't ready to hear. "Might not hurt to ask her."

"There's nothing *to* figure out," I countered, wrapping my arms around myself. "I didn't ask for any of this." The memory clawed its way back— zealots surrounding me, Karyseth's venomous words, blood slipping down my skin onto that damned altar. A shudder rippled through me, bone deep. I crossed my arms tighter. It wasn't enough to hold the memories at bay.

Selene's gaze softened, but she didn't argue. Her elbows rested on the table as she watched me in that unnervingly steady way medics had. Like she wasn't just treating wounds but cataloging whatever might linger beneath. When she finally spoke, her words cut straight through my defenses. "And yet, here you are, sitting in his tunic, spilling over with more anger about liking him than the fact he nearly tore a priestess to shreds to keep you safe."

The floor felt suddenly unstable beneath me. I opened my mouth to deny it, but no words came out.

Damn her and that disarming precision.

"Look ... I'm not saying you need to declare your undying devotion after four days. But maybe instead of running from what's happening as fast as you can, sit with it. Decide what you actually want, not just what's easiest."

I leaned back, wary. "You think this is easy?"

"It's easier than admitting he matters." She nodded toward the tunic I was fidgeting with, a faint, teasing smile brushing her lips. "He's right there, on your skin, and you're fighting him tooth and nail."

I groaned, pressing both hands to my forehead. "He's not just overwhelming. He's ... consuming. He looks at me, and ..." My voice broke slightly, the heat rising to my cheeks as I remembered how Rath's eyes blazed when he called me *shyrarva*—like I was the center of everything his world revolved around. "He's so sure, like he knew this was inevitable. And I —I don't *get* how that feels real."

She stood quietly, her fingers returning to sort through folded bandages. "If this is going to be your reality, you'll need to decide sooner or later if Rath is part of your plan. Because from what I've seen?" She smirked faintly. "He's already made his choice."

Her words hit me harder than I wanted to admit. I slouched deeper into the chair, stubbornly tracing the carved heat veins lining the wall. Despite my hesitation—and outright denial—something kept pulling me toward him, as inevitable as a current in rushing water. But I refused to put that into words. Refused to let her see my hesitation grow roots.

"I should get going. Kira's probably five loaves deep into baking mode," I said, forcing a weak laugh as I stood, brushing off the details too big to face directly.

"You mean before Rath realizes you're gone and goes scorched earth on the city to find you?" Selene quipped smoothly, already stacking supplies back onto her shelves.

Her comment stopped just short of teasing, but it still nudged too close to reality. I waved her off and let myself out, the door clicking softly shut behind me.

The tunnels were quieter now, the soundscape reduced to the occasional hiss of steam vents far above. The market district lights had probably dimmed by now, and I imagined the bustling trade had slowed to murmur and flicker.

But Selene's questions still churned. What role did I want Rath to have in my life? *Did* I want Rath in my life? Did any of it even matter? The bond couldn't be broken. We were stuck on this planet. What choice did I even have?

My thoughts spiraled violently as I walked. Time moved strangely in Scalvaris with the suns blotted out by so much rock, it was difficult to keep track. When I reached the tighter corridors leading to Rath's quarters, the silence weighed too heavy. Something chafed against my instincts, the kind of subtle wrongness that set alarms I couldn't ignore.

The corridor felt empty—but not the kind of empty that invited peace. The eerie sort, like the silence of predators just before striking. Heat crystal veins faintly lit the walls, painting jagged shadows across the passage floor, their occasional flickers betraying any movement.

My heart thudded faster. Each step felt heavier. My fingers flexed reflexively at my sides, searching for something to anchor to as the unease crawled across my skin. If someone was following me, I didn't want to confirm it by turning.

Then, just ahead, the shadows wavered unnaturally before solidifying into a hulking figure.

Drakarn.

I stopped breathing for half a heartbeat. Dark scales glistened against the crystal's dim light, their edges marked with dark red burns that'd fused them jagged near the warrior's left jawline. His wings hung poised, their membranes catching barely enough light to seem like a predator fanning them before striking. All menace. His slitted eyes warmed with barely contained hostility as his snout lifted to fix me under his unwavering scrutiny.

I knew him. One of Karyseth's zealots—Krazath. Those burns hadn't been there the last time I'd seen him.

The hate in his eyes? It had only grown stronger.

This was *so* not good.

SIX

ORLA

My feet were lead.

My fight-or-flight reflex leaned toward panic in both directions, but escaping through the narrow passage the towering Drakarn now filled wasn't an option.

If Krazath wanted me dead, running wouldn't do me any good.

I couldn't let him think I was weak. If the Drakarn were one thing, it was brazen. I couldn't be a meek little human. My voice came low, steady enough—though too sharp-edged to be safe. "Nice burns. Someone cooking a little too close to the lava vents?"

His sneer widened, with fangs catching the faint light. "Foul human," he rasped, his voice scraping like charred stones grinding against each other. His claws flexed as he crept forward, his tail dragging along the floor. "You crawl among us, stinking, frail ... You should be extinguished like vermin."

I squared myself, forcing calm into my stance even though I doubted it would last. "You're wasting my time." Stupid. Taunting a zealot was idiotic, reckless even.

But something hot inside me couldn't be cautious. Not right now.

I think I really hate this guy.

Krazath's eyes narrowed, his yellow pupils contracting into sharp slits. Heat radiated from him, thick and stifling. His tail struck the ground with a crack that rolled through the stone like thunder.

"You, and all your kind, pollute this place," he spat. "Soft, brittle things who scavenge at the feet of real power. You stand here because one of us allows it. Because the warrior lord is too blind to see what filth he's bathed himself in."

"Funny," I said, my voice steadier than I expected. "Considering you're spending your time cornering one of us *weakings*, I'd say you're the one dragging down the honor of your people. Picking on me doesn't make you powerful. It makes you pathetic."

Real smart, Orla. Poke the dragon some more.

Krazath's lips curled into a snarl. "Watch your tongue, *mokral*," he said, his claws raking across the stone wall. My translator couldn't handle that last word, but the tone was clear that it was an insult. "Rath's protection won't last forever. It's made a mockery of everything. No Drakarn worthy of their name allows himself to—" His sneer deepened, the next word practically spat from his mouth. "*Mate with prey.*"

The insult hit me harder than it should have. I clenched my fists at my sides, the urge to lash out bubbling in my chest. My rational mind screamed at me to shut my mouth, to stay quiet, to de-escalate. But another part of me, that deep-seated fire Rath had somehow stoked, refused to back down.

"He doesn't seem ashamed to me," I bit out. "But if you have such a problem with him, why not take it up with Rath directly? Oh, that's right—you won't, because you'd lose. Badly."

The words left my mouth before I could weigh them, and the reaction was immediate. Krazath's eyes flared with rage, his tail slamming against the wall with enough force to send tiny fractures racing across the surface. It was getting hotter with every passing second, like a freaking furnace.

"You frail, arrogant worm," he hissed, taking a step forward. His wings flared slightly, casting long shadows down the passage. "You think you're untouchable because he chose you? Tell me, human, what will you do when this bond proves false? When the council strips him of his honor for this shame he's branded on himself?"

I gritted my teeth, taking an instinctive step back. The passage behind me was narrow, the walls rough against my fingertips, but there was no escape route. Krazath kept advancing, his hulking frame growing larger with every moment.

His tail lashed out again, brushing against the stone near my leg, close enough to send pebbles flying. My breath caught in my chest, panic dangerously close to winning out, but I refused to give him the satisfaction of showing it. My instincts screamed for help, but there was no one to hear me—not here. Not now.

The roar came like an eruption, not just loud but thick and guttural, shaking the air around us. The sound hit me in the chest, a physical force that reverberated down the passage.

Rath.

His shadow spread over us, massive, looming, impossibly huge. Krazath froze, his snarling confidence melting into something almost comically scared. Rath landed between us, wings unfurled, claws flexing at his sides with deliberate menace. His yellow eyes blazed, locking entirely on Krazath.

"Do you value your life so little that you'd dare threaten her?" Rath growled, the words a rough snarl that carried more weight than any shout could. Each syllable carved itself into the air, vibrating with intensity.

Krazath's wings twitched, retreating closer to his body. His composure cracked, though his own snarl remained, however dimmed. "I've done nothing to your human." His voice carried an edge of defiance. "But I will not hold my tongue. She doesn't belong here."

Rath's tail lashed sharply. He took a step closer, each movement deliberate, his wings brushing the walls as his presence swelled to fill the corridor. "She belongs where I say," he rumbled. "You've overstepped."

Under other circumstances I might have felt bad for Krazath.

Almost.

The tension between the two Drakarn was tangible. Rath's fury was a living, breathing thing, so heavy in the air I felt it pressing against my skin.

But Krazath wasn't done yet. He straightened, baring his fangs in a last-ditch show of bravado. "Your bond is a disgrace," his voice rose dangerously. "You weaken yourself by clinging to a creature so far beneath us. The council will not let this stand forever. Even you cannot—"

The motion was faster than I could track. In a blink, Rath's claws were at Krazath's throat, his tail coiled sharply around one of the other warrior's legs to keep him pinned. The force of his movement sent heat crystals shuddering.

Krazath froze, his wings pinned awkwardly against the stone as Rath pressed him into the wall. The tips of Rath's claws barely dented Krazath's scales, but it was enough. The promise of what they could do lingered in the air.

"You forget yourself," Rath snarled. "I have claimed her. The bond has been witnessed. Speak against it again, and you won't walk away."

Krazath stiffened, refusing to flinch despite the claws hovering near the vulnerable seam of his throat. "Kill me here, and you lose what little respect you still have." He had to strain to speak.

Rath didn't move, the menace radiating from him crackling in the air like charged embers. His claws flexed ever so slightly, enough to make Krazath's neck strain even harder against the pressure. Every muscle in Rath's body screamed restraint about to snap, held in place by a force of will barely tethered.

He wasn't going to back down. I wasn't sure he *could*. But I had a sinking suspicion Krazath was right.

"Rath."

The single syllable breached the suffocating silence. He didn't turn immediately, his wings still flared, chest rising and falling in bursts. But my voice had reached him. Slowly, his head shifted, eyes now more orange than yellow locking onto mine. They burned sharply, though beneath the fury ran something deeper—conflicted, something raw.

I took a cautious step closer, my pulse beating so fast and uneven it was dizzying. "Don't," I said, my voice quieter this time. "He's not worth it."

Rath's tail remained coiled, his claws unmoving. Then, with a deliberate exhale, Rath shoved Krazath back against the wall and released him.

Krazath stumbled, quickly regaining his footing, though his entire body bristled with humiliation. He glared at Rath, his wings twitching, itching for retaliation. But he didn't dare make a move.

"You forget yourself, Flame Heart," Krazath muttered, voice dripping with venom. His gaze flicked to me, the disdain in his expression twisting my stomach. "This will not end well for you. Or her."

Rath's growl vibrated through the stone floor beneath me. "Leave. Now."

Krazath's eyes narrowed, but he held his tongue. Slowly, he retreated into the shadows, his claws scraping along the basalt wall until his shape dissolved into the distant gloom.

Silence filled the corridor again. The weight of everything hung around us, choking away the air as my pulse thudded in my ears. Rath still hadn't moved. His wings remained half-spread, his shoulders locked and tense, even as Krazath's form grew distant and then disappeared entirely.

All at once, my knees felt weak, and I leaned against the cooler wall for balance, dragging in sharp breaths. The corridor shrank around me—heat, emotions, fear, everything collapsing inward. But it wasn't *just* fear. I looked at Rath, at every line of tension in his frame, and saw something more than rage.

I found my voice, barely a whisper. "He's gone."

Rath didn't react immediately. His tail snapped behind him, short, tightly controlled arcs that betrayed his lingering agitation. It wasn't until I took a hesitant step closer, this time letting my fingers hover inches from him, that his focus shifted. He looked at me, and the edges of that predator's fire softened just a little.

"You're shaking," he said, his voice rough—hoarse, almost tender in its uneven delivery.

My whole body trembled, from adrenaline, from everything that had just happened. One hand clasped the fabric of my tunic. I was breathing too fast, too shallow. I was trying to ground myself, but the room still felt unsteady.

Without a word, Rath moved. Fluid. Deliberate.

In a single step, he closed the space between us, his massive hand landing softly against the small of my back while his tail wrapped securely around my legs. For a creature so imposing, his touch was shockingly careful, almost reverent. He pulled me toward him, the heat of his chest pressing into me like a shield against the world. His claws shifted, hesitant, before curving over the back of my head.

"You're safe," he murmured, his voice brittle, like the words were more for himself than for me. "No one will touch you. Not while I breathe."

The dam inside me broke. Hot tears spilled over before I could push them down, frustration and relief colliding in a way that was too much to hold in.

My fingers gripped the loose fabric of his tunic as my forehead rested lightly against his chest. There was no fighting it—no pushing him away even though some part of me insisted I should. I hated the comfort I found in his presence, hated that it settled me better than anything else.

Hated that I didn't pull away.

The tears came harder, and Rath didn't try to stop me. He held me close, his tail tightening just slightly to anchor me. His thumb brushed gently over my shoulder.

"Let it go," he said.

I shook my head weakly, voice muffled against the smooth scales of his chest. "I didn't ask for this."

"Neither did I." He was quieter now, laced with a kind of rawness that caught me off guard. His words hung there, heavy and unshielded.

I tilted my head to meet his gaze, expecting deflection or annoyance, something calculated. Instead, I found that same flicker of vulnerability— the crack running under all the searing confidence he projected. It did something to me, tugged at threads in my chest I didn't realize were tied so tightly.

"Why do you care so much?" The question escaped before I could stop it, more honest than I intended. I regretted it instantly. Surely, he wouldn't—

"You're mine," he said simply, like the answer was carved deep into his bones. His gaze burned, unrelenting in its certainty. "No one will touch you. Not Krazath. Not anyone."

I blinked, the weight of his words pressing into the space between us. His voice carried no hesitation —just absolute conviction. It terrified me. Not because of the possessiveness, but because something in me wanted to believe him.

I snorted unsteadily, trying to mask the twisting warmth in my chest with something sarcastic. "Humans don't exactly subscribe to this 'fate-bonded forever' thing, you know."

Rath tilted his head. "Maybe that's why you shatter so easily," he said, not cruelly, but with a faint edge borne of an observation he couldn't possibly have made. "You're too quick to let go."

It should've annoyed me. It didn't. Instead, it settled somewhere deep, pulling at parts of myself I didn't want to examine.

Finally, I sighed, wiping the last of my tears with the back of my hand. "This won't stop them, you know," I said quietly. "The zealots, the council, Kary-seth. They're not just going to let this slide." My voice faltered slightly, gesturing toward the corridor where Krazath had disappeared.

Rath's wings folded at last, his body slowly losing its tension. He stepped back half an inch—but only half. "Then let them come." His voice crackled with the threatening promise.

I groaned, thumping my head against his chest. "That's not an actual solution."

His lips twitched—not quite a smirk but enough to send that sharp curve of a fang glinting faintly. "It's the only one they'll understand."

I shook my head, torn between exasperation and something dangerously close to trust. "You're impossible."

His tail brushed briefly against my back before curling faintly near my feet again. "So are you."

The faintest, reluctant smile tugged at my lips. Maybe impossible wasn't so bad.

SEVEN
RATH

The Blade Council's private chambers were near-silent, punctuated only by my claws drumming against the polished table. The room was cavernous and foreboding. No flames burned in the sconces—just the cool glow of heat crystals embedded in ancient walls. Normally, I found purpose in the hush, its weight sharpening thought and honing words. But now, all I could focus on were the whispers.

"... your bond is a disgrace ..."

Krazath's taunt clung to me, acid and unshakable. The effort it took not to rip his throat out still thrummed in my veins. I'd lost my temper before, but never so closely to losing full control. The memory of Orla's voice cutting through that red haze—steady, soft—kept me from digging my claws into the stone right now.

"If you scowl any harder, Rath, your face might stick that way."

Vyne's voice shattered the silence. He reclined in his chair, green scales catching the dim light. That smirk of his was always too wide, the gleam in his gaze constantly daring someone to test him.

"Careful," I warned. "You might tempt me to see how quick you really are."

His smirk only grew. "Bold words. Aren't mates supposed to mellow old warriors? You sure you shouldn't be off romancing your human instead of sulking like a fledgling?"

Heat crawled into my chest, roughening my tone. "And what would you know about mates, besides imaginary ones you put into terrible poems?"

A loud crack cut me off—Khorlar's fist crashing down on the table. His granite-gray scales looked dull, but that glare of his had enough force to still anyone.

"Enough," he said, voice like grinding stone. "If you wish to quarrel, do it elsewhere."

Vyne raised his hands in mock surrender, though mischief still danced in his eyes. I tamped down my anger with effort. He wasn't entirely wrong—my mind had been wandering all morning, and I hated that fact.

Darrokar finally spoke from the head of the table, where he'd sat in silent observation. Faint red pulses played across his black scales as he tapped his claws on the armrest. His voice held the weight of both his status and his role as my oldest ally and friend.

"We don't have time for squabbles," he said. "Your bond with Orla has thrown the council off-balance. Half see it as a betrayal of our ways. The others view it as proof of your strength in taming a wild creature. Either way, the whispers aren't stopping."

I bared my teeth, the tension building in my chest. "Let them whisper. Krazath, Karyseth—whoever challenges me will regret it. Besides, you have a human mate. They accepted her."

Darrokar's brow arched. "You've already nearly taken Krazath's head off, if the rumors are accurate. News of that is everywhere. And as for my mate, you were out on scout duty when I made my case. This new match has reignited all the resistance I faced."

Khorlar folded his broad arms, drawing my attention. "He's right. You may not have killed Krazath, but you almost did—and that's enough to stir trouble."

My anger flared again. "I won't hold back if someone threatens my mate. And Krazath is telling tales. I barely touched him."

"Be that as it may," Khorlar said calmly. "Your actions have fallout. Krazath is nobody, but his allies wait for you to lose control."

Every detail of last night was etched into my mind: Krazath cornering Orla, how her fear laced the air, how rage nearly consumed me. Only her voice had kept me from ripping his throat out.

Darrokar's deep tones cut in, "You're on a blade's edge, Rath. The council was wary enough of letting the humans stay. There are plenty who respect the Forge more than you, even if they are not adherents."

I usually would have argued, but Darrokar's words held too much truth to dismiss. I could feel the weight of them like a blade pressed to my neck.

"I will not let her go," I said, voice edged.

"Of course not," Darrokar snapped. "You need to be smarter. You built your place here through victories; win this battle the same way."

Khorlar nodded. "The people remember your strength in the River Trials, and how we took care of those lava beasts the Narvix tried to unleash on us. You can sway opinions, but not if you act like a mindless brute whenever your mate's involved."

I hated agreeing with them, but a seasoned part of my mind recognized the logic. The fire inside me, though—the one that began the moment Orla entered my life—raged at the thought of placating anyone who'd undermine her.

Vyne's drawl cut in again. "Maybe spend a little less time in bed with her and a little more time proving you're not going soft."

I shot him a glare that made his grin waver. He would never stop laughing if he knew I did all of this for a mate I had yet to even kiss. One taste had made me *this*.

When she finally opened herself fully to me ...

I couldn't think of that here, especially not now.

Darrokar rose, his towering shape casting a long shadow. "No one doubts a bonded warrior who makes his mate's protection part of his strength," he said, "but you must prove it isn't a weakness. The River's Run Festival is coming up," he said. "The timing couldn't be better."

"For what?" I asked, wary.

He met my gaze without flinching even though his words were a knife. "For you and Orla to participate in the Mating Challenge."

The tension in the chamber thickened so much I

could barely breathe. Vyne whistled softly. Khorlar's stony brow furrowed, but he remained silent.

I stared at Darrokar, anger igniting behind my ribs. "Absolutely not. No one's done that in years. Surely you jest."

He shook his head. "Never about this. You know the festival's importance; they still speak of your success at the warrior trials all those years ago. The Mating Challenge is revered—our people treat it as the ultimate test of bonded pairs."

I felt my wings twitch, my pulse hammering. "It's insane. Warriors spend years preparing to face it together. She's a civilian. And a human. You think I'll throw her into a crucible meant to break the strongest among us? I don't see you offering to throw your human in beside mine."

"Tread carefully now," Darrokar warned, the beginnings of a growl under his words. "If you can't find some way to prove the bond to the doubters, this will not end. Zealots corner her while your back is turned. Word spreads that your human mate weakens you. Is that safer?"

I let out a long breath, claws curling into the table. "You think risking her life solves this?"

"I think showing the council—and all of Scalvaris —that your bond is more than a ploy to protect her is the only way. The River's Run draws every eye. If they see your mate stand at your side, if they see what she's made of, they'll have no choice but to accept her."

"She's human," I said in a low rasp. "You expect her to pass a challenge designed for trained warriors, ones who can brush off wounds she cannot?"

Darrokar's expression didn't shift. "I've seen what these humans can do. They're stronger than many care to admit—and you know it too, or you wouldn't have claimed her."

That truth sank like a hot coal in my gut. Orla was fierce in ways few understood. But she hadn't chosen this life. It had chosen her. I couldn't make her face such trials purely to appease the old guard. Yet ... I saw Darrokar's point. Too well.

I forced my shoulders to relax. "And if I refuse?"

Darrokar's gaze hardened. "The doubt will continue to spread until Karyseth finds a way to truly challenge you in council."

Drakarn traditions were harsh. A mate bond was supposed to be sacrosanct. Lying about it would dishonor a warrior beyond nearly all else. I wasn't lying, but a small part of me could understand why it might look that way.

Vyne's voice drifted back into the stalemate.

"You could always make another public declaration. Challenge someone for her honor, take her right there in the marketplace—very dramatic. The city will love it."

I turned on him with a snarl, tail whipping the air. "Try me, Vyne."

Khorlar broke in. "He may be a fool, but he's not entirely wrong. Your woman must know the stakes. If she accepts, at least the council won't treat her as a human outsider—they'll treat her as your mate."

A brittle kind of hope mingled with dread in my chest. Orla wouldn't shy from a confrontation. She'd meet it head-on, even if it tore at her. The thought of exposing her to the Mating Challenge, though, made my blood chill.

"Let me talk to her," I ground out, not hiding my reluctance. "She deserves a choice. I have taken enough from her already."

Darrokar nodded. "Good."

I pivoted sharply toward the exit, wings fluttering in frustration, tension climbing my spine. I'd had enough of this.

Khorlar's rumbling voice stopped me mid-stride. "Don't forget why you chose her."

I didn't turn around. Couldn't. The memory of that primal pull, the way her scent sliced through me and stirred something feral, flashed again in my mind. Conviction and fear tangled in my throat.

One false step and I'd pay in Orla's blood.

The corridors outside felt stifling, the veins of heat crystals pulsing along the dark walls. My steps echoed louder than normal, each stride a release of pent-up energy I couldn't unleash in the council room.

Then I saw that piece of filth—Krazath. He smirked as he spoke in hushed tones with Zarvash, another councilor and a follower of the Forge Temple. Krazath's wings were partially unfurled in an agitated stance, while Zarvash's calm expression gave nothing away. When they noticed me, their voices dropped even lower.

I let my steps slow, eyes narrowed. Their posture —leaning in, wings tense—reeked of plotting. I caught a stray sentence from Zarvash: something about opportunists and precarious positions. Typical.

Zarvash stepped away from Krazath and inclined his head as he passed me. "It seems I cannot go a day without hearing about you."

I grunted. "And you believe it all?"

His bronze eyes flicked over me, unreadable. "I merely follow the truth. Wherever it may lead."

He moved on, leaving Krazath to glower at me

from the edge of the passage. I stared back, letting him see the warning in my eyes.

If he tried coming near Orla again, I'd finish what I started.

My tail lashed behind me as I marched on, refusing to engage. Whispers were turning to poison, the wind in Scalvaris carrying rumors that sharpened like blades. If I stayed idle, they'd come for Orla the moment they sensed weakness.

I wasn't slow or soft. I'd walk straight through a wall of flame for her.

But the Mating Challenge? That might be a step too far.

Something would break soon, and I'd damn well make sure it wasn't her.

EIGHT

ORLA

The combat arena vibrated with an energy that sank into my bones, an undercurrent of heat and expectation that made the air feel electric. It wasn't just noise or movement—it was this pulsing vitality, as if the cavern was alive, fueled by the clash of blades and the rhythmic pacing of trained warriors.

I leaned forward on the rough-hewn stone bench in the observation area, the grit beneath me scraping against the thin fabric of my tunic. My presence here felt wrong—a guest in a moment that wasn't mine—but I was too curious to resist.

That, and Rath had asked.

"Here, try this," Eden said, pressing closer to my side as she handed me something wrapped in foil.

"Earth candy. Save me before I scarf it all down myself."

The cheerful, fluorescent colors on the wrapper were almost outrageous in this environment—like smuggling daylight into shadows. I lifted an eyebrow at her, but her grin was irrepressible, her dark brown eyes bright with the kind of humor that disarmed you before you knew it. Eden's energy was like standing too close to a sparkler, irritating and charming all at once.

"Your heroism knows no bounds," I replied dryly, taking the candy. The foil crinkled as I unwrapped it. The candy hit my tongue like a slap of concentrated sweetness, the fake fruitiness coating everything in a way that felt nearly alien after weeks of consuming krysfruit and slabs of burnt meat.

"You're welcome," Eden said, popping a second piece into her mouth with a dramatic snap. She leaned forward, her elbows resting on her knees as her gaze swept over the warriors below. "Which one's Rath?"

I scanned the pit, my eyes darting from winged figures to shimmering scales, searching for that particular sharpness that had become so familiar. Swaying tails twitched, claws glinted, and blades thick with heat refracted dim light until finding him in the crowd felt impossible.

Then it wasn't.

That moment when I spotted Rath was like swinging a door open too fast and catching a blade of sunlight. My thoughts snagged because this wasn't the Rath I was used to—not the watchful, tightly-coiled man who spoke with clipped words and calm truths. No, this figure moved with an effortless swagger that made something deep inside of me tighten with want.

Oh, hell.

"How could you miss him?" I heard myself mumbling. His imposing frame cut through the chaos. Other warriors were strong, brutal even, but Rath's presence was something distinct, an unfamiliar language of danger and grace—power in its rawest form. His scales reflected light like shards of glass, catching every flicker of motion in a way that created a halo of shimmering, restless energy around him. His wings unfolded slightly; not wide, but calculated, like a wolf showing just enough teeth to let you know it wasn't interested in playing nice.

"Never mind," Eden said in awe, her voice breaking my spell as she zeroed in on him. "Found him. Seriously, though, your guy could probably walk into a room and set it on fire just by existing."

Heat crept up my throat, uncomfortable and unwelcome. "He's not my guy." I wasn't sure if the words were meant to rebuff her or convince myself. Feeling Eden's sidelong glance, I sighed and forced a casual shrug, but the movement felt unnatural, wrong. "He just ... knows how to make himself seen. That's all."

Eden turned her half-smirk my way for just a second too long. "Sure," she said, her voice dripping with disbelief. Her posture instantly melted back into something more casual as she leaned forward again, resting her chin on one hand. "But seriously, that presence. Like, if someone so much as looked at me the way Rath looks at you ..."

I groaned, cutting her off as she dragged the words out like each one had worth in its own right. "Eden. Please."

She smiled, lifting her hands in a playful gesture of surrender. "Fine. Commentary off. But the fact that you're still red? Not my fault."

In the arena below, Rath advanced on his sparring partner—a warrior whose movements began with confidence but quickly transformed to hesitation. Rath's blade didn't move like the others, didn't try to impress. It sought efficiency.

Watching him was like watching the beach grind down stone: violent and inevitable but removed from petty emotion. Even the air around him seemed different, a slight stillness in the invisible space between moves that put spectators on their heels.

It wasn't theatrical. It was purpose built for destruction.

"Doesn't hold back, does he?" Eden asked. Her earlier levity had dimmed, replaced by something quieter.

"No," I replied, swallowing hard. My hands clutched the edge of the bench. "He never does."

The arena's collective breath sharpened, a break in the rhythm below turning all focus toward the latest fight. A new challenger stepped forward, taller and sharper-edged than the others—his scales jagged and mismatched, singed in a way that made him seem more like something built imperfectly than born.

Krazath.

Eden stiffened at my shoulder instantly, her fingers curling into fists. *"Him,"* she hissed before exhaling sharply. "That asshole."

I knew. Recognized him from the corridor, from

the temple, from the tension Rath had worn like armor since. My pulse stuttered, uncertainty and rage colliding somewhere too deep for me to untangle. Despite myself, I leaned forward.

"No," I breathed, watching Rath turn to meet Krazath's gaze—a fire already sparking in his eyes. He didn't hesitate, didn't flinch. He entered the space of Krazath's challenge like it was inevitable, like this confrontation had always lived in their bad blood.

Krazath's first move was a sweeping strike, the kind meant to intimidate and overwhelm—a predator testing the weak points of his prey. His blade arced through the air, but Rath was already moving, his form a blur of red and shadow, slipping to the side with a fluidity that made Krazath's lunge look clumsy by comparison.

Rath's counterattack came swiftly, his blade slicing upward in a motion so precise it seemed choreographed. Krazath twisted away just in time, the edge nicking one of his jagged scales instead of cleaving through flesh. The sound of it—a sharp, metallic scrape—sent a shiver down my spine, and I gripped the bench under me so hard my knuckles ached. Or maybe it was the fight itself, the suffocating tension coiling tighter with every traded blow.

Eden's voice dropped lower. "He's claiming you. That's what this is, right? Showing everyone that you and him ...?"

Her words knocked against me sideways, almost disorienting. "That's ... insane." Part denial, part something that sounded a bit too much like hope.

"Isn't it?" she said, but her focus was unwavering. "And yet, here we are."

Rath's style was deliberate, measured—a predator who wasted no energy. Every flick of his claws, every step forward or back seemed calculated to expose Krazath's weaknesses. Krazath fought like a storm, wild and frantic, each strike more aggression instead of strategy. His scales caught the dim light, flashing like broken glass as he swung again and again, trying to break past Rath's cold precision.

When Rath ducked beneath a violent down-swing, his wings snapped outward in a sudden motion. It was a feint, but Krazath took the bait, stepping left where Rath's foot was already planted. Rath spun, low and fast, his tail whipping around to strike Krazath's shin with bone-cracking force. Krazath stumbled, snarling in frustration and pain as he caught himself on one knee.

"Come on, Rath," I whispered under my breath, my voice lost in the roar of the arena.

I hated this. I hated watching what looked like a car crash. My throat felt raw already, like I'd been screaming even though I'd been biting those yells back as hard as I could. But beneath my concern, there was a dark, treacherous part of me that wanted Rath to humiliate Krazath, to crush him so completely that whatever thread of malice still tied him to Rath would snap. I wanted—I needed Rath to win, because losing wasn't an option. Not here. Not with Krazath.

Krazath recovered with a roar, his jagged claws swiping at Rath in a wide arc that forced him back a step. But Rath immediately surged forward again, blade aimed for Krazath's ribs. The two were locked in close combat now, claws and fangs snapping as their bodies twisted in a brutal struggle. Rath locked one of Krazath's wrists in a vice-like grip, twisting with a sharp motion that forced his opponent to drop the secondary blade he'd been brandishing. It clattered to the ground and skidded away into the dirt.

For a heartbeat, Rath's face tilted upward, and our eyes met.

It was only for a fraction of a second, but the ferocity in his gaze hit me like a tidal wave. It wasn't hesitation or desperation—no, Rath wasn't just here to survive. He was here to finish this, to make an example of Krazath.

I couldn't look away even as my hands trembled, my nails digging into the stone beneath.

"Damn," Eden's voice was almost inaudible. "He's ... something else."

But my attention was back on the pit, my chest tight as Krazath fought back with a vicious headbutt, the crown of his jagged scales slamming into Rath's cheek. Rath staggered, and Krazath surged forward like a wounded beast sensing weakness. My heart jumped into my throat as Krazath's blade lashed out, aiming for Rath's unguarded side.

Rath's wings flared wide at the last possible moment, snapping him back and away from the attack. Krazath's blade sliced only air as Rath rose into the space above their clash, hanging there like some radiant, damnable god of war. Then he dove, his descent like a meteor aimed directly at Krazath's chest. The impact landed with a deafening crack as Rath's claws wrenched Krazath's weapon from his hands and sent it spiraling away. The crowd roared, their voices blending into a singular chaos as Rath's blade pressed to Krazath's throat.

The fight was over. Everyone knew it. Even Krazath.

It took another few minutes for Rath and Krazath to observe the formalities. Krazath limped away towards a bronze scaled Drakarn who was glaring at Rath. But I couldn't care about that. Not right now.

I jumped out of my seat and scrambled down the steps towards the floor of the arena like I was some fan at a hockey game back on Earth.

"Rath!" My voice rang out, rebounding faintly off the stone walls of the arena.

Ahead of me, his steps faltered. I watched his tail dip in its usually measured sway, the movement slower now, as though the storm of emotions from the fight below was still rattling inside him. His shoulders remained stiff, wings tucked tightly against him, but tension rolled off him in waves.

I pushed forward, quickening my steps until I'd almost caught him. My fingers brushed the dark fabric of his sleeve—a fleeting touch that made him freeze instantly. His wings twitched, the faint, sharp motion betraying that coiled energy he barely contained.

Slowly, he turned to face me.

And then there were his eyes.

I wasn't sure what I'd expected—anger maybe. But when Rath looked at me, it wasn't fury I found crackling behind his gaze. It was something softer, quieter, but no less powerful. A tension of a different sort tightened across the planes of his face, his jaw locked like he was holding back a torrent of words he couldn't quite put to shape. The intensity of it sent a surge of heat traveling up my spine.

"You were ..." I faltered, shoving the words around in my head before one finally fell out into the silence. "Incredible."

I felt the weight of the admission as soon as it left me—a truth I couldn't take back even if I wanted to. My face burned under his scrutiny, the heat of my words hanging awkwardly between us. But I held his gaze, hoping somehow my honesty would cut through whatever wall he was throwing up right now.

Rath watched me like he was studying every fragment of my face, looking for cracks in my reasoning. Then, slowly, his expression softened—not a lot, but enough that the hard lines of his features eased, and the tension in his shoulders bled away just a fraction. His hand moved—just slightly—as though he wasn't sure whether to reach for me or retreat, claws flexing faintly before settling by his side.

"You are unharmed?" he asked at last, his voice rasping like sandpaper scraping over stone.

The question caught me off guard. "I—you're the one who was fighting! Not me."

His jaw twitched as he exhaled slowly through his nose, a dark and indecipherable flicker passing behind his eyes. But then he shifted slightly closer—a small movement, enough that I could feel the faint warmth of his skin, even through the layers that separated us.

"It was for you," he said simply. "They needed to see."

Something inside me wavered. The world felt too small all of a sudden. The sharp edge in Rath's voice didn't match the softness of his gaze as he studied me. His quiet admission—words that rang with pure honesty, untempered and raw—coiled in my chest, making breathing inexplicably difficult.

"I—" Words failed me as my thoughts got all tied up. My lips parted in an attempt to say something—anything—but before coherent language could rally itself, some shared thread between us tightened and snapped clean through.

I kissed him.

NINE

ORLA

It was instinctual—messy and unplanned, like something breaking through a dam you'd ignored was cracking all along. My hands had moved without permission to brace against his chest, my fingertips instinctively brushing the heat rolling beneath his tunic. His skin, warm like heated stone, burned against me in a way that made my stomach twist.

I barely registered the way his breath stopped short, the faint hitch of it ghosting across my cheek. And still, I couldn't stop.

Everything ground to a halt. Rath didn't move, caught mid-instinct and undecided about which way to fall. His hands hovered in that uncertain space between grasping and retreating, claws curling tight against his palms. For a second, I wasn't sure if I'd gone too far, crossed a line I didn't fully understand, until—

Until he moved.

Slowly, deliberately, Rath leaned into the moment with a care that bordered adoration. If the kiss was meant to break him open, it did so in increments—his lips firm but measured, like he was unlearning and relearning the world in the span of seconds. He tilted his head faintly, matching me, and just when I thought the storm between us was only a distant rumble, his hand found my waist.

The sharp heat of his claws, even through the protective layers of fabric, sent a shiver racing across my body. His grip was firm but careful, aware that the strength he carried so effortlessly could crush if miscalculated. The other hand came up too, fingers grazing my jaw with a touch so tender it left a trail of fire.

For all his capacity for destruction on the field, Rath kissed like he was holding something fragile. It undid me completely.

An involuntary sound escaped me—a quiet tremble fought and failed to be smothered. Rath stilled for only a heartbeat before a low hum rumbled deep in his chest, that faint growl a visceral reaction that spoke more than words ever could. The weight of it pressed against me, made every small tether anchoring me to reality snap.

There was no disguising the hunger threaded into his kiss—the way his lips moved more firmly now, with just enough edged desperation to make my heart stutter and spiral all at once. His grip tightened against my waist as his other thumb grazed just along the edge of my face. The warmth radiating from his skin enveloped me completely.

Time didn't exist between us. There was no measured counting of breaths, no acknowledgment of anything beyond the persistent, magnetic pull binding me irreversibly to him.

When Rath finally pulled away just enough to breathe, the space between us felt fragile, the air charged with something that hadn't yet settled. His forehead brushed lightly against mine, unwilling to pull back completely, and for a fleeting moment, we both stood frozen in that sizzle. His eyes burned with something unreadable, raw and unguarded in a way that tightened and softened my chest all at once.

He exhaled, the hint of warmth in his breath lingering against my lips. "*Shyrarva*," he rasped, that word catching somewhere low in his throat, vulnerable and rough-edged.

I couldn't respond. Couldn't move. Because the

look he gave me wasn't just intense—it was exposing Rath's inner soul, daring me to step into the chasm I'd just forced open.

"I—" The syllable was barely audible; a ghost of a word that dissolved the moment I uttered it.

My voice had betrayed me, my thoughts racing too fast to form anything coherent. I tried again, but the tightness in my chest stifled any clarity, leaving me breathless and trembling in a way I couldn't control. My hands slipped from where they'd been clutching at his tunic, retreating awkwardly to my sides.

Rath didn't speak. He stood motionless for a moment, caught between moving closer and pulling away entirely. His gaze dropped to my lips again before sweeping back upward, catching and holding mine with the same intensity that had turned my pulse inside out moments ago. When he finally stirred, his hand didn't fall away. Instead, his thumb lingered at the edge of my cheekbone, brushing the curve of my skin with an unexpected gentleness that made my core clench.

He leaned in slightly—just enough for his lips to ghost across my temple in a gesture so soft it was almost imperceptible. The whisper of contact was there and gone, but it left a weight in its place. His claws flexed once at his side before stilling again.

"You ..." His voice, rough and deliberate, dropped low. "Taste sweet."

It wasn't flirtation, not really. Rath wasn't posturing—he was simply delivering an unfiltered truth. A fact, delivered the way one might observe a shift in the wind or the steady glow of a distant star. And yet, those three words sunk their claws into me with far more force than anything practiced or contrived ever could. They left me reeling, tangled in sensations I hadn't quite found the nerve to name.

I swallowed hard, helpless against the flush that crept up my neck. My head dipped slightly, instinct pulling me away from the direct line of his gaze in a feeble attempt to collect myself. "It's the candy," I muttered, the excuse spilling out too quickly, too obviously, as if the absurdity of it could dissolve the gravity of what had just happened.

"The candy," Rath repeated, his tone edged with faint amusement, but it wasn't dismissive. If anything, his voice sounded lighter now, less hesitant. He watched me steadily, his head tilting slightly to the side. A faint curve played at the corner of his mouth, subtle but unmistakable—less a grin and more the shadow of something that might've been softness, had it belonged to anyone else.

"Yes, the candy," I insisted like it mattered. "Artificial sugar, weird additives. Science, or ... something." My hands gestured vaguely, but even I didn't believe the excuse as it left me.

His breath left him in a quiet huff—not an outright laugh, but close enough to trail warmth through the space between us. He took a step back, the movement so measured it felt less like retreat and more like careful consideration. His eyes didn't stray from mine, still holding steady in that way that sent sparks tracing along my nerves, even as the distance afforded me some scrap of relief.

The return of the background noises—whispered murmurs from lingering Drakarn nearby—felt abrupt, like the outside world had forced itself back into focus before either of us was ready for it. I wasn't sure what was worse: the crowd's judgement-lined gazes or the lingering hum in the air from Rath's proximity, charged despite the subtle distance now between us.

"Let's get out of here," Rath said, voice quiet but resolute. "The stares will only grow heavier." His hand, still steady even as mine trembled faintly by comparison, extended forward—an invitation rather than an assumption. "Away from this."

For all my hesitation, my fingers brushed against his without thinking, drawn forward more by the weight of his presence than any conscious decision on my part. His touch was steadying, a quiet guide away from the turmoil still echoing through the arena.

In a swift motion, Rath stepped closer, his arms and tail wrapping securely around me as his wings spread wide. The rush of movement that followed—the leap into the air—stole my breath as the ground disappeared below us. His strength, the sheer solidity of him beneath and around me, was grounding in a way I hadn't expected.

As the city's sprawling depths gave way to the open expanse of sky, a new kind of quiet settled around us—thicker, calmer, where the muted roar of the wind carried no judgment or expectation. I leaned into him, the warmth of his scales blocking out the cool bite of the wind, and my stomach flipped in a way that had nothing to do with the flight.

It wasn't until we began aiming for the soft, glowing light of a familiar space nestled high above the city that I understood where he was taking me.

"Your sanctuary," I murmured, my voice tinged

with something quieter than awe but no less full of wonder.

Rath tilted his head slightly, glancing back at me just as the sanctuary's crystalline shimmer began to catch and reflect the light. "Yes," he said softly, matter-of-fact as always, but with a deeper purpose stitched into the single word. "It is what you need." His wings flexed once as we descended fully, slowing to land gracefully on the secluded cliffs below.

When my feet found solid ground again, he didn't step away, not immediately. Instead, his gaze lingered, searching for something—I wasn't sure what—but finding some answer all the same.

I didn't look away.

The air in the sanctuary shifted the moment we landed inside. It looked the same as before—the light filtering delicately through the overhead openings, scattering soft reflections across the pools dotting the cavern floor. But there was something different about it now, some newfound weight in the silence, heavier and more profound than the first time I'd been there. I stood just past the entrance, my fingers skimming the rough stone, and let the space breathe around me. The tension in my chest eased.

Rath moved farther inside, his wings pulling tight against his back, steps uncharacteristically careful. He didn't look back at me, at least not right away. Instead, he let out a breath, the sound carried away by the quiet.

Here, in this place, his usual sharpness seemed muted. Not absent—Rath was never truly at ease—but less rigid, his presence more thoughtful and drawn inward. He paused near one of the pools, his back to me, his head tilting slightly in the way it did when he was weighing something unspoken.

I hovered near the entrance, reluctant to disturb the fragile peace unfolding before me. My hand lingered on the stone for a moment longer before I forced myself to step forward, movements slower than his, less sure. The sanctuary's beauty pressed softly into my awareness, an ache of something I couldn't quite name settling beneath my ribs.

"Rath," I murmured, his name slipping through the quiet.

At the sound, he turned to face me. He didn't speak immediately, studying me with that unyielding intensity that seemed to see too much. His tail flicked slightly against the ground, a motion that betrayed whatever storm lingered beneath the surface. When the silence stretched just enough to become awkward, I forced myself to step closer, drawn forward as much by the heat of his gaze as by some need to fill the void.

I stopped a few paces away, my arms crossing over my chest as I tried to steady the unease knotting between my lungs. "I don't understand why you're doing this," I admitted, the words emerging unpolished, trembling slightly on their way out. "Why you care so much."

Rath's posture shifted, but his expression didn't falter. If anything, his gaze softened slightly, though it carried the same depth. He said nothing for a long moment, his head tilting faintly, weighing whether I was truly ready to understand the answer.

His claws flexed absently at his sides before his voice broke the stillness. "Your world," he began, his words deliberate, unhurried. "Your people. You've lost much. I see it in you. The way you carry it."

His honesty sliced through me, sharp and unavoidable. My breath hitched slightly, and I tightened my arms across myself. Rath had always been direct, but this felt different—less like an observation and more like a confession.

"I know what it means to lose," he continued, his tone quieter, a faint roughness creeping into its edges. His gaze shifted, no longer fixed rigidly on me but staring somewhere past the pools that flickered faintly with light. "My sister ... she was fierce. Brilliant. Everything I was not." A pause lingered between his words, thick and heavy as memory pressed against them. "And then she was gone."

My throat tightened. Rath was standing there, unraveling pieces of himself in a way that left me breathless. My voice was thready when I found it again. "I'm sorry."

He shifted his gaze back to me then. "Sorry won't bring anything back," he said softly, though there was no anger in the words—only a quiet kind of resignation. "But I am sorry too, for what you carry."

The rawness in his voice undid something in me. In the span of heartbeats, the carefully constructed barriers I'd built around my grief wavered, threatening to collapse entirely. I took a small step closer, unsure of what I was reaching for but needing to close the gap between us all the same.

"You don't have to shoulder that alone," I said, surprising even myself with the quiet conviction in my voice. The words felt foreign on my tongue, unfamiliar but true.

Rath's claws flexed again—a small motion, but one I recognized now as a sign of his restraint cracking. "I will not lose this," he said finally, his voice rough, his gaze steady as it pinned me in place. "Do you understand?"

I swallowed hard, his words—and the meaning behind them—settling heavy in my chest. "Rath," I started, the syllables too small for the enormity of what surrounded us. "I—"

But Rath shook his head, cutting me off with a look rather than words. "Stop running," he commanded, the simplicity of it unraveling me in ways I hadn't thought possible.

My heart twisted painfully at the honesty etched across his face.

How long had I been doing just that—running? From losing my future, from the shattered remains of what I'd left behind, from the truth of what existed between us now? The enormity of it settled around me, and I didn't know how to answer; didn't know how to step into the space he'd so carefully made for me. But I wanted to try.

Rath's hand found its way to my waist again, not gripping but resting there in a way that tethered me to him, grounding me when my thoughts threatened to spiral. It was steady, solid, and patient. "May I?" he murmured, voice low and edged with hesitation as his eyes flickered briefly downward, lingering on my lips before meeting my gaze once more.

"I want to kiss you now. When no one else is looking."

I nodded, a small motion that sent everything else tumbling out of the way.

When his lips found mine again, it wasn't with the same urgency as before. His warmth spilled into me as his claws skimmed along my side, careful and reverent. I let him in, let the storm of everything that had bound me up dissipate in the face of quiet, unrelenting truth.

Whatever this was, I wasn't running anymore.

TEN
ORLA

I sat cross-legged on the edge of Rath's bed, my fingers tracing the intricate weave of heat-resistant silk beneath me, when the door slid open with a quiet scrape. Things had changed since the cave, since the kiss. Kisses.

I was starting to feel more comfortable in Rath's rooms. Our rooms. I didn't shy away when he looked at me like he wanted to devour me. And I cherished the few stolen kisses we'd shared since then. It wasn't some seismic shift in our relationship.

But things were different. Maybe even better.

Rath clutched a small cloth pouch in one clawed hand. The scent hit me first—sweet, floral, *rich*—cutting through the room's usual musk of charred stone and spice. My stomach betrayed me with a low growl.

Rath's nostrils flared, a flicker of satisfaction tightening his jaw as he stepped inside. "You're hungry," he said, not a question.

"I'm fine," I lied. Old habits.

He grunted, unimpressed, and crossed the room in three strides. The pouch landed on the bed between us with a soft *thud*, its contents shifting like treasure. Up close, the scent was dizzying—caramelized sugar, something nutty, a hint of flowers.

"What is it?" I asked, eyeing the pouch like it might hiss.

His tail flicked impatiently against the floor. "Open it."

I tugged the drawstring loose, and the aroma bloomed fully—honey, hot oil, crisp dough. Nestled inside were six golden brown fritters, their surfaces crackled and glazed, still faintly steaming. My mouth watered.

"You ... got these? For me?" I blinked up at him, surprised.

He shifted, the scales along his neck rippling faintly. "You favor sweets." A statement, blunt as a blade. "The vendor claimed these were ... sufficient."

Sufficient. The word felt too small for the effort. I

plucked a fritter from the pouch, the pastry's heat seeping into my fingertips. The first bite was a revelation—crisp shell giving way to airy dough, the honey inside hot and floral, tinged with a smoky aftertaste that could only be Volcaryth. A low, involuntary moan slipped out.

Rath went very still.

I froze, the sound hanging between us like a spark. His pupils narrowed to slits. "You ... approve?"

"It's delicious," I admitted, licking honey from my thumb. His gaze tracked the movement, a muscle twitching in his jaw.

Without warning, he sank onto the slab beside me. His thigh pressed flush against mine, scales warm through the thin fabric of my pants. My breath hitched.

"Here." He plucked the fritter from my hand, claws sheathed as he broke off a piece. His other hand cupped my chin, tilting my face toward him. "Eat."

I parted my lips, and he placed the morsel on my tongue, his thumb lingering to catch a stray drop of honey. The pad of his claw grazed my lower lip, sending a shiver down my spine.

"Good?" he rumbled.

I nodded, swallowing hard. "Why ... why this?"

His thumb swept over my chin again, snaring another streak I hadn't noticed. "A warrior honors his mate's tastes." The words were rough. "Even … small ones."

A laugh bubbled up, startled and warm. "Small? There's enough here for three people."

The corner of his mouth twitched—not a smile, but close. His tail rose from the floor to loop loosely around my ankle, a possessive anchor. "Eat," he repeated, offering another piece.

This time, honey dripped down my thumb as I took it. Rath's nostrils flared, his gaze dropping to the sticky trail. Slowly, giving me plenty of time to pull back, he leaned in.

His tongue—long, hotter than human—flicked over my honeyed skin.

I gasped. The sound seemed to fracture something in the air.

Rath froze, his breath a low rasp against my wrist. For a heartbeat, we stayed locked there, the world reduced to the glide of his tongue and the gleam in his eyes. Then, with a growl that vibrated through my bones, he pulled back.

My pulse thundered in my ears as I reached into the pouch with trembling fingers. The fritter's crust crackled under my grip, scattering sugar crystals across Rath's scales. His tail tightened around my ankle—a warning or encouragement, I couldn't tell.

"Here, have a taste," I managed, breaking off a ragged piece.

His nostrils flared at the offering, gaze flicking between my face and the crumbling pastry. For a heartbeat, I thought he'd refuse. Then his lips parted, revealing the faintest glint of fang.

The moment the morsel touched his tongue, his pupils blew wide. A low rumble shook his chest as flavors exploded—honey's floral brightness against Volcaryth's smoky depth. His clawed hand engulfed mine, preventing retreat.

"More."

The command vibrated through my bones. I fed him another piece, then another, each bite punctuated by the slick heat of his tongue grazing my fingertips. His scales glowed faintly where our skin met, marks blooming under my touch like stars being born.

When the last crumb disappeared, he didn't release my hand. His tongue swept the length of my index finger, rasping over calluses left by rock samples and scanner grips. The sound that escaped me was half gasp, half whimper.

"You taste," his growl deepened, tail coiling higher up my calf, "like sunlight."

His eyes trailed down, snagging on the exposed skin of my upper arm. I usually kept it covered. "What is this?" He traced the inked lines swirling across my inner forearm. The constellation patterns seemed to shimmer under his touch, dormant stars awakening beneath scaled fingertips.

I swallowed. "Cygnus. Lyra. Ursa Major." My throat tightened around the names. "They're constellations."

His clawtip hovered over the swirling colors of the Milky Way. "And this?"

"Home." The word slipped out raw. "Or where home used to be. Before ..." I gestured vaguely toward the ceiling, toward the sky that didn't exist there.

Rath's tail tightened around my thigh, the pressure grounding. "Show me."

One by one, I guided his claws over each cluster of stars tattooed on my arm, my voice gaining strength as I recounted myths half-remembered from childhood datapads.

"This one bled," he observed, talon brushing the faded blue ink.

"My first tattoo." I huffed a laugh. "Twelve-year-old me thought stealing a biogel pen from the medbay was a genius idea."

Rath made a sound deep in his chest—not quite a chuckle, but something warmer than a grunt. "My Blade-Binding." He turned his forearm, revealing a jagged scar cutting through ruby scales. "Fifteen summers. Stole a magma whip from the forge master." His claw traced the injury with perverse pride. "It took three healers to seal the wound. I kept the whip."

His tail slid higher, scales scraping against my legs as he nosed aside my hair to expose the honey-smeared hollow of my throat.

"Your stories are written in dead light," he murmured against my pulse. "Mine in fire."

The star on my arm felt like it was pulsing faintly, keeping time with the possessive grip of his claws. Somewhere in the heat, a new constellation was being born.

Rath's claw closed around the half-empty pouch with wicked deliberation, his gaze locked on the honey glistening at its torn edge. The low light caught the golden strands stretching between fabric and talon, each thread snapping with a soft *pop* that echoed too loud in the sudden stillness. His nostrils flared—inhaling sugar, heat, *me*—as he leaned in until his breath fanned hot across my jaw.

"This," he rumbled, "belongs here."

The pouch tilted.

"Rath!"

Honey spilled in a ribbon, thick and sticky, painting a warm trail from the hollow of my throat to the slope of my breast under my shirt. I gasped at the heat—not scalding, but alive, like sunlight given liquid form. It pooled in the dip of my collarbone.

Rath's tongue swept over a fang. "Better."

His free hand settled at my hip, claws pricking warning-dimples into flesh as he leaned closer. The honey's floral scent mingled with his own—charred cedar and midnight embers—as the last drops fell. His thumb followed the viscous path upward, smearing it wider, *darker*, until my pulse throbbed where honey and his touch collided.

The empty pouch dropped to the floor. His other hand caged my wrist above my head, scales hissing against stone as he lowered his mouth to the mess he'd made.

"We can't let this go to waste," he said. His slit pupils drank greedily at the honey dripping over me. "Too many layers," he growled against my throat.

The first rend of fabric came without warning. His talon hooked beneath my shirt's neckline, slicing downward in one fluid motion. Cool air rushed over newly bared skin as the garment fell away in forgotten scraps. I arched instinctively, honey-smeared breasts heaving under the hunger blazing in his eyes.

"Mine."

The declaration vibrated through his chest and into mine as he straddled my hips. He tore off his own tunic, ruby scales glinting beneath, nipple piercings catching the crystal's glow. My brain short circuited at that.

The first lick was a brand.

I barely registered the cool air on my exposed stomach before his tongue struck—a hot, flat stroke from collarbone to pulse point that left scorched nerves in its wake. His teeth grazed skin, not breaking flesh but promising consequences.

When his mouth closed over the honey pooled in the hollow of my throat, the vibration of his groan traveled straight to my core.

"It tastes better here," he rumbled against damp skin, that wickedly long tongue flicking the frantic beat beneath my jaw. His hips ground down, the rigid heat beneath his trousers leaving no doubt about his state. The musk pouring off him thickened —smoke and charred amber with an undercurrent of something sweetly metallic.

I had to touch him.

He hissed when my nails caught the black hoops piercing his nipples, the sound sharpening as I rolled one between thumb and forefinger. "You," his claws tore through the remains of his trousers, letting the fabric fall to the floor, "play with fire, *shyrarva*."

The honey between us grew tacky as he reared back, allowing me to see what I'd uncovered. Thick liquid leaked out of the head of his cock. A barbell through his foreskin glinted wetly, each subtle twitch making the pierced flesh quiver like a living thing.

He was pierced *there* too.

Oh my god.

My breath stuttered. Human anatomy hadn't prepared me for *this*—the way red scales rippled like armor at the base before melting into swollen crimson flesh, dark veins pulsing beneath the surface.

Thick. *Too* thick, my hindbrain whispered even as heat pooled between my thighs. The foreskin didn't just pull back—it *rippled,* a strange lip curling lazily against the glans, glistening with beads of translucent fluid that carried his smoky-sweet scent.

My mouth watered.

The barbell piercing through it all caught the light, swinging faintly with every twitch of that alien flesh.

"It's ..." I swallowed, fingers flexing uselessly at my sides. "Not what I expected."

Rath's tail lashed once, violently, before coiling around my bare calf. "Displeasing?" The growl held an edge I'd never heard—vulnerability masquerading as threat.

"No." My hand moved without permission, hovering inches from where pre-cum slicked the veined shaft. "Not even a little."

A claw caught my wrist. "*Shyrarva.*" The word was a lit fuse. When I met his gaze, the hunger there scorched every clinical thought to ash. "Touch me."

It wasn't a command. It was desperation.

The first brush of fingertips against his scaled base drew a hiss from us both. The ridges weren't cold—they thrummed with inner heat, textured enough to tease without tearing. Higher up, the skin turned velvet-soft, the dark veins beneath thickening until they felt like braided cords under my palm.

That writhing foreskin lip curled around my thumb when I reached the crown, suckling gently.

Oh god. What would that feel like inside me? My body clenched with curiosity and need.

"*Karynae,*" Rath gritted out, hips jerking. His pierced flesh quivered, more fluid welling around the barbell. The musk intensified—clove and burnt honey now, *claiming* pheromones that made my mouth water even more.

All thoughts of science evaporated. There was only heat, and need, and the terrifying realization that I *wanted* this alien intimacy. That every scale and throbbing vein called to something primal I'd buried under data logs and survival protocols.

His claws sank into the silks around us as I stroked him properly, the tongue-like ridge undulating against my palm in counterpoint to my strokes. "Your science," he rasped, fangs gleaming, "did it prepare you for *this?*"

The barbell grazed my wrist as his hips pistoned, the answer written in my racing pulse.

His tail lashed once before slithering up my inner thigh, the tip leaving ghostly trails of sensation. "This scent," he growled, dragging his nose along my honey-smeared ribs. The motion pulled his cock away from my curious hand. "Your fear. Your hunger. They sing the same note now."

The first lick to my nipple drew a broken sound from us both. His tongue's ridges pressed almost too hard, the tip curling around the peak in a way no human mouth could replicate. When his cock's fleshy lip brushed my inner thigh—hotter than the rest of him, questing blindly—I arched off the bed with a cry.

"Look," he commanded, pinning my hips as his tail wrenched my leg higher. The glide of his cock's extra tongue circled my clit while the rest of him pressed against my entrance, the barbell's cool metal a shocking contrast to the searing flesh around it. Twin sensations splintered my vision into starbursts. "Watch how you take me."

The world narrowed to points of contact—the searing press of Rath's scaled leg against my inner thighs, the sinful undulation of that alien ridge circling my clit, the cold-warm shock of metal where his barbell kissed my entrance. His claws flexed against my hips, pinning without bruising, as his tail coiled higher to keep my leg in place. It should have felt restraining; instead I felt safe. Every shift of muscle beneath his red scales rippled with lethal grace, a predator holding itself in check.

"Breathe," he growled against my ribs, the command fraying at the edges.

I sucked in air that tasted of honey and him, my fingers scrambling for purchase on the bed's silks. The first breach burned—not with pain, but with obscene fullness, the barbell dragging a slick path inside me as his writhing lip latched onto my clit. My back arched off the slab, a cry catching in my throat as dual sensations collided—deep, stretching pressure below and fluttering suction above.

"*Karys'veth ir,*" Rath snarled, words rumbling through his chest into mine. I had no idea if my translator was malfunctioning or if I was just too lost in sensation to understand what he was saying. I couldn't care.

His hips snapped forward, seating him fully in one sure thrust. The scaled base of him ground against me as his veined shaft pulsed, his cock's tongue working in counterpoint to each jarring movement. My vision whited out, nerves howling as the tip of his tail traced the outside of my thigh.

"You feel—" He choked off, fangs scraping against my shoulder. The mark walked the knife's edge between pleasure and pain, his tongue lapping at the sting as his pace turned erratic.

The relentless feeling pushed me over. Pleasure

crested like lava breaching a vent—a scalding, unstoppable rise that shattered into full-body tremors.

Rath's roar vibrated through my bones as my climax clamped down on him, his tail seizing around my thigh as his own release surged hot and thick. The scent of us—charred amber and honeyed musk—swelled until it coated my tongue, his glands marking my skin where his seed spilled.

He collapsed forward, catching his weight on trembling arms, his forehead pressed to mine as I gasped uselessly at the heated air. His cock still pulsed inside me, milking the last aftershocks as his tail loosened its vise grip.

"*Shyrarva.*" That word, his special name only for me, was a prayer and a plea on his lips, his claws gently carding through my sweat-damp hair.

I traced the marks my nails had left on his back—constellations of possession barely marked in his scales. His answering rumble sounded almost like contentment.

Rath's weight pressed me into the silks, his forehead still resting against mine, our shared heat forming a humid little world between our bodies. Honey had dried in sticky trails across my chest, mingling with sweat and other fluids. His tail remained coiled around my thigh, a possessive anchor even now.

His pierced nipples brushed my chest with each labored breath, the hoops now warm from our friction. "You're trembling," he murmured against my throat, his voice sandpaper rough.

A claw-tipped hand slid beneath my lower back, adjusting our alignment until his softening cock slipped free. I bit back a sound at the loss, suddenly aware of the mess we'd made—his release seeped between my thighs, thick and unnervingly warm, carrying that musky-sweet scent that already felt branded into my skin.

Rath's tongue dragged a slow stripe up my honey-crusted collarbone. "Mine," he growled, the word muffled against my skin. Not a question.

I should've bristled. Instead, my traitorous hands fisted in the silks as his teeth found the juncture of neck and shoulder. Not biting—*testing*.

"You're *smug*," I accused, hating how breathless I sounded.

His answering rumble shook through me, more purr than growl. The tail around my leg tightened fractionally as he nosed aside damp hair to lick the shell of my ear. "You smell like me now."

A shudder went down my spine. "Is that ... a good thing?"

He stilled. Drew back just enough for me to see the way his pupils dilated—black swallowing gold. "It means," he said slowly, claws flexing against my hip, "that even the zealots will think twice before challenging what's etched into your scent."

The implication coiled hot in my gut. *Pheromones as property claim.* I opened my mouth to protest, but Rath's thumb brushed the bite mark on my shoulder —the one that throbbed in time with my heartbeat.

"Hush." His nose traced the honeyed hollow of my throat, inhaling deeply. "Your mind will dissect it later. For now," his hips rolled once, a lazy undulation that made me gasp, "let the fire speak."

I wanted to argue. To dissect the biology of his "scent-marking glands," to question the permanence he implied. But his hand was sliding lower, calloused palm cradling the back of my knee, and the words dissolved into a moan.

Somewhere in the fervent quiet, I realized my fingers were carding through the ridges along his spine, memorizing their topography.

Rath's breath hitched, and his hips bucked.

I stilled. "Did I—?"

"Again," he demanded, voice cracking.

This time, when my nails scraped the sensitive grooves between his scales, his whole body shuddered—a seismic vulnerability that echoed in the broken sound he muffled against my throat.

The fire spoke.

And for once, I listened.

Orla's breathing was soft against my chest. The air was thick with the scent of her—my scent now woven into hers, permanent and undeniable. I didn't need my heightened senses to notice how perfectly it clung to her skin.

Even in sleep, her body carried the mark of our bond.

A low hum of satisfaction rumbled in my chest. She was there, pressed against me, her fragile human frame fitting perfectly against mine as if the stars themselves had shaped us for this. For each other. My tail tightened its lazy coil around her bare thigh, and the warmth of contact kept threats and doubts at bay for precious moments longer.

She shifted slightly, and I froze. Her face turned

toward me, her lashes brushing her cheeks where the glow from the heat crystals danced faintly against her skin. Even now, grappling with the fragility humans wore so openly, I could feel it beneath the surface—the core of strength she didn't see clearly in herself.

The sight of her like this—unguarded, peaceful—should have soothed me entirely. But as my claws brushed idly over her shoulder, tracing one of the curling tattooed designs etched into her skin, I felt the truth simmer deep inside. It threatened to unseat the quiet victory coiling in my chest.

She was fragile in ways a Drakarn would never be. Soft skin where scales should have grown, bones that lacked the tempered strength of volcanic rock. What would stop the world—the council, the zealots, Karyseth—from taking her away from me? What if ...

I tensed, drawing in a slow breath, too measured to be casual, unwilling to let her feel my unease. Damn it. The thought still lingered, twisting cruelly under the protective satisfaction radiating through me.

It wasn't that I doubted her strength. Quite the opposite—I'd seen it flash like lava-forged steel when she squared her shoulders despite fear, when she spoke truths I didn't want to hear but needed nonetheless. I'd seen it in the fire of her defiance, in the way she'd bled and fought for survival in a world so utterly foreign to her.

No, it wasn't her I doubted. It was the bond—or her perception of it. Did she understand what it meant to me? To us? Or did she still see it as temporary? A convenience? A circumstance she'd never intended to become entangled in?

The thought burned more than I cared to admit.

I rolled onto my side, careful not to disturb her, and propped myself up on one elbow. My gaze swept over her form, soft curves barely concealed by the remnants of the sheet tangled at her waist. Her arm stretched beside her head, bearing lines of ink I now recognized as part of her own fragmented mythology —a map of home, of hope, impossibly distant.

A human thing—this need to carry their past like scars and trophies.

I traced another constellation on her forearm, the faint texture of raised skin under my fingertips a startling contrast to my own hardened scales. Her tattoos spoke of stories written in stars long dead, far from the volcanic flames that forged Drakarn bodies and culture. Both beautiful, but worlds apart.

Possession stirred again, heavy and insistent in my chest. She was mine. The bond was everything, absolute, undeniable in its truths. She belonged in this place, with me, and yet ...

Fear dug its claws in. What if it wasn't enough? What if she didn't want to stay?

I growled low under my breath, the sound rumbling more ferally than intended. Her eyelids fluttered slightly, and I forced myself to still, reigning in the breadth of emotion threatening to spill over.

She shifted against me, her head nuzzling faintly into my chest, lips parting with the softest sigh. One of her hands slipped upward, brushing the side of my rib cage. A simple movement, unconscious even, but it sent a warmth spreading through me sharp enough to drown out the darker thoughts lingering at the edges.

Her breathing shifted, soft sighs turning into faint murmurs as she began to stir. I watched the transition, the way her brows knit slightly before smoothing, how her lips parted in confusion or dream and then settled again as her body woke slowly. Each micro-expression felt like a revelation, a glimpse into the depths of her humanity that both fascinated and confounded me.

The rising heat in my chest softened into something gentle, tender. Adoration claimed me, an urge old as the volcanic rivers of Volcaryth—protect, cherish.

I leaned down, brushing the faintest kiss against her temple. A small shiver rippled through her, but she didn't wake fully, so I pressed another kiss lower, to the delicate line of her jaw, the corner of her mouth. Her soft scent filled my senses, tinged now with the unmistakable marks of me—of us.

She sighed, her lips curling into something that was almost a smile, her eyes still closed as though resisting wakefulness. My tail tightened its coil faintly, holding her closer, savoring the way her warmth fit perfectly into mine. I trailed my claws lightly along her exposed side, careful not to nick or scratch, though my instincts stirred sharply at the sight of her bare skin.

"You're awake," I murmured, my voice softer than I'd intended, vibrating low against her ear.

She made a noise between a hum and a breath-less laugh, her eyelids fluttering open as her eyes found mine. "Barely."

"You sleep heavily," I teased, shifting my head so our foreheads brushed, my horns curving enough to frame her face without touching.

Her lips quirked, though her voice was still

heavy with lingering sleep. "Maybe I finally found the right pillow."

I swallowed, my claws stilling against her skin as I searched her half-lidded gaze. I wanted to ask her why this moment, why me, but the weight of the sentiment filled the space between us louder than any words could.

Instead, I let action speak. I dipped my head and kissed her. Not the fire of the night before, but something slower, deeper, a language closer to worship. Her breath hitched in surprise, but she melted into it, her fingers sliding up my chest to rest against one of the ridges glowing faintly at my throat.

I let out a low sound of approval, my palm spreading over her lower back as I pulled her closer. Her body responded instinctively, arching slightly into mine, her warmth soaking into my scales. My tail flexed again, securing her in a loop of heat and pressure that felt more protective than possessive.

She was mine, and everything in me wanted her to know it without question.

Her hands slid higher, grazing the edge of one nipple piercing before meandering up to curve lightly over my shoulders. The fire began to rise again, building as my lips trailed lower, testing the length of her neck to indulge in her pulse there.

Every small whimper, every hitch of her breath flared the bond between us tighter, hotter.

"Rath," she said my name softly, her voice somewhere between a warning and an invitation.

I pulled back just enough to meet her gaze, my own breathing heavier now, a faint growl slipping loose before I could leash it. "You taste like sunlight," I rumbled, echoing what I'd told her the night before. A lazy smile tugged at her lips, though it faltered slightly as I traced the side of her throat with my tongue, unwilling to break the connection entirely.

My claws flexed faintly against her waist as I forced my breathing to steady, the bond humming between us taut as a bowstring. She was there, and I would indulge in her forever if it were only up to me —but it wasn't. Not entirely. The council's whispers, the scrutiny of the zealots, Krazath's venomous words—they all lingered like shadows, encroaching on the sanctuary of this moment.

I kissed her forehead softly, lingering just long enough to imprint the gesture into my memory, before pulling back. "There's something we need to talk about."

Her eyes narrowed a fraction, shifting from the sleepy warmth of moments ago to something sharper.

"That sounds ominous," she said carefully, her voice tinged with curiosity but underlined by caution.

I sat up slowly, shifting her against me so she remained within my reach, still curled in the protection of my tail. My claws tapped absently against my thigh, weighing words against the storm beginning to churn inside me. "The River's Run Festival begins in four days."

She blinked at the abrupt shift in tone, her brow furrowing faintly. "Okay ... And?"

I met her gaze, letting the weight of my own seriousness seep into the air between us. "It's one of the most crucial events in Scalvaris," I began, my voice low and steady. "It's not just a celebration; it's tradition, culture, strength. It's ... everything."

Her brows arched at my tone, but she said nothing yet, her full attention now locked on my face. I hadn't lied—she was perceptive, almost frustratingly so. I pressed forward before doubt could creep in.

"There is a ... challenge," I said, the words feeling heavier as they formed. "The Mating Challenge. It's a trial set to prove the strength, the harmony of bonded pairs. Any warrior who has claimed a mate can participate, and to succeed is to remove doubt and silence whispers." The words hissed through my teeth. "Like the ones circling us now."

Her silence stretched just a moment too long for comfort, her expression unreadable. She sat up more fully, drawing the frayed sheet higher against her chest as if the motion could shield her from what I was asking.

Finally, she spoke, each word precise. "You're telling me you want us to compete? Publicly, in front of the entire city?"

I forced myself to stay still, to keep my claws from flexing too visibly. "Yes," I said. "Not just for them. For us. To solidify what we have—to show *everyone*—what this bond means." My voice softened slightly, though I knew my words still carried hard edges.

If this was the way to keep her, then I would do it. I could make sure she was safe. No one would doubt us again.

She exhaled sharply, pushing her wild hair out of her face with one hand. "Rath," she began, her tongue catching her lower lip as it always did when she was preparing to say something uncomfortable. "Do you hear what you're saying? This sounds ... dangerous."

"It is," I admitted, not shying from the truth.

"But you're capable. And I would never let anything happen to you."

Her head tilted slightly, her gaze sharpening to an almost surgical precision as she studied me. "This isn't just about proving something to them, is it?" she asked quietly. "You're trying to prove something to yourself."

The words sliced through me. For a moment, I couldn't speak, my throat tightening around the denial that refused to form. She didn't give me the chance to find whatever honesty I could muster.

"Rath," she said again, firmer this time. "I ... I need to think."

And before I could stop her, she slid out of the bed and walked away.

TWELVE
ORLA

My mind was a fragmented mess, thoughts colliding like spent debris in orbit, falling and burning before anything meaningful could take shape. I stayed in Rath's quarters just long enough to dress, my movements sharp and mechanical, as if forcing my body into motion could quiet the storm of my thoughts.

It didn't.

Last night lingered as if it had physically etched itself into me—every touch, every growled vow and promise, every searing kiss. As thrilling as it had been, as natural as it had felt to succumb to the pull between us, the aftermath now beat with heavy uncertainty.

Fated mates.

Bonding.

His claim that I was his. The very idea bristled against every logical bone in my body. It should have felt ridiculous, laughable even.

How was I supposed to reconcile my concept of love and connection, something I'd always believed to be built slowly, steadily, with the Drakarn belief of an instant, primal bond dictated by pheromones and instincts?

Except it wasn't ridiculous—not in the way his eyes had burned into mine last night, like I was all that mattered in his world. Not in the way his presence felt stitched into the air I breathed, as if some invisible string tethered us together whether I wanted it or not. Not in the way I'd felt that crushing pull in my chest when I saw him lock eyes with that bastard Krazath in the arena and knew that he'd stepped into that fight for me.

My hands shook as I laced up my boots. I forced myself to pause and focus, fingers gripping tightly to the leather straps.

What the hell was I doing?

Rath was emotionally ... consuming, that much was obvious. But what shook me was how much of myself I'd already given over in return. Since crashing on this volcanic hellscape, my life had been a string of survival-based decisions: solve the next problem, fix the next broken thing, keep yourself and the team alive.

Somewhere along the way, Rath had become one of those problems—or perhaps he'd convinced me survival meant hiding myself in him like he was my armor.

But now? After last night—after talk of some crazy mating ritual, laid out so plainly this morning—none of this felt simple anymore. The problem wasn't just Rath or me or the bond itself—it was all of it, twisting together in this impossible, dizzying knot of biology and circumstance that no Earth training manual could prepare me for.

"Shit." My knees hurt from kneeling too long, the stone floor unforgiving even through the thin layer of fabric covering my skin. I pressed my palms against my thighs to ground myself, willing my frantic heartbeat to slow.

Rath had given me space. I had no idea when he would return to this room and, frankly, the thought of facing him right now put a lump in my throat—not from fear, but from the unbearable pressure of how much he just ... expected from me.

Not demanded, exactly, but Rath's intensity didn't leave space for half-measures or hesitation. If I stayed, if I said yes to him in every way that mattered, there would be no turning back.

And I wasn't sure if I could live up to that.

I needed more space. I needed time to think—somewhere Rath wouldn't follow. He had to sense my turmoil, I was sure of it, but if I left before he returned, maybe I could buy myself just enough distance to wrestle my thoughts into something coherent.

Outside, the whirr of distant voices and the rush of the river carried on, too ordinary to care about my internal conflict.

How could something so monumental happen, and the world just ... keep turning?

The corridors twisted and opened, the spaces feeling labyrinthine and growingly familiar as I navigated them on autopilot. I wasn't even sure where I was going until the faint sound of rushing water reached me, the humid air thickening as the path sloped downward. My chest ached with too many emotions to name, and instinct guided my steps more than reason.

The baths.

I didn't know why the thought brought the promise of relief, but it was enough to pull me forward. I needed calm, clarity—anything to cut through the riot in my head and heart.

Not to mention, I was still a bit … sticky.

The baths were one of the few places I'd found since arriving here that still felt … soft. Even with steam hissing from the walls like the breath of unseen leviathans, and algae casting the water in ghostly hues of green and blue, the space was undeniably alive in a way that soothed the edges of my anxiety.

I stripped my clothes in the small changing area and chose a pool in an alcove where prying eyes were unlikely to watch. The warm air clung to my skin as I slipped into the water, the heat enveloping me immediately and drawing a groan from my throat.

It was hotter than I'd expected, almost scalding, but the sting soothed after a moment, replaced by a deep warmth that seeped into my muscles and began to soften the tension I'd been holding onto for so long.

Steam curled in lazy tendrils around me, drifting toward the stalactites above. The algae-infused light kissed the water's surface, rippling faintly with each exhale I released into the mineral-rich pools. Beneath the surface, the volcanic stone was smooth under my feet.

I closed my eyes and sank lower until the water lapped at my shoulders, letting the heat absorb some of the weight pressing against the walls of my chest. For a moment, just a fleeting moment, I tried to pretend I was anywhere but there. That I was back on Earth, immersed in some sort of secluded hot spring, with no alien trials or fated bonds to unravel and no piercing golden eyes haunting me.

But Volcaryth didn't let me forget itself. The ever-present trace of fire lingered in the air, a sharp reminder that I was far removed from the world I'd called home.

The idea of *home* twisted something in me, a deep, confusing ache that I'd been suppressing since the moment we crash-landed. I had thought I'd come to terms with it, that I'd made my peace with the idea that Earth—my colleagues, my family, the life I'd left behind—was gone. But there, in the quiet of the baths, it all bubbled back up.

Maybe that was what terrified me the most about Rath and everything he represented. I wasn't just fighting against this bond—I was fighting against what it might mean to give up the ghost of the life I used to dream of.

Rath wasn't part of that dream. This world wasn't part of that dream.

And yet, somewhere deep within me—far deeper than science could probe—something in me wanted him anyway.

I pressed my palms to my face, the heat from the water clinging to my skin as I inhaled deeply through my nose. The steam burned slightly on its way into my lungs.

I was startled from my spiraling reflection by an unmistakably human voice, sharp and warm as it pierced through the haze of steam.

"Mind if I join you, or are you hiding?" Selene's voice floated toward me before her figure resolved through the mist, a towel wrapped around her body. Her long black hair was damp, clinging to her skin. She must have just emerged from another pool.

I managed a laugh, though it carried a hollow edge I couldn't quite disguise. "I'm hiding, but not from you. Maybe cowering."

Selene grinned, but the look in her dark eyes was searching. Without waiting for more permission, she sank into the water near me with a soft sigh, the ripples from her entry washing over me.

"You've got that look," she said as she settled in, leaning back against the smooth stone edge casually. "The one that says your whole world just got turned upside down. Or exploded."

Her bluntness sent a derisive snort escaping from me. "Can't it be both?"

"It absolutely can," Selene quipped, offering me an easy smile as she swept her fingers through the water. "I'd argue they tend to go hand in hand. Want to share?"

I hesitated, bracing myself. Selene had always been disarming in her no-nonsense approach to everything—from patching up wounds to sassing intimidating alien warriors—but I wasn't entirely sure even she could make sense of this.

Still, the words began to tumble out before I could stop them. "I feel like I've stepped into a story I don't understand," I admitted, my voice low and thin against the cavern's hush. "And somehow I've already committed to roles I didn't ask for."

Selene tilted her head, her sharp gaze softening just a fraction. "This about Big Red?"

My laugh cracked this time, barely holding together. "When isn't it about him? And don't call him that."

She huffed, sending a ripple of steam-laden breath across the surface of the water. She nudged my leg with her foot under the water, a gentle prod to pull me from my spiraling doubts. "I'm guessing this is less about Rath the warrior and more about Rath the ... whatever he is to you?"

I swallowed hard, trying and failing to dislodge the knot in my throat. "He thinks I'm his fated mate," I said softly, the words tasting almost bitter on my tongue. "And maybe ... maybe there's something chemical or biological there, something real. But it's all so ... fast. So overwhelming. And I've barely figured myself out here, let alone what I am to him."

Selene was quiet for a moment, her gaze sliding toward the faintly glowing pools farther out in the chamber. Her words were gentle but purposeful.

"I won't pretend to understand it all. Kaiya and I have been trying to wrap our heads around the biology. The pheromone stuff, the bonding rituals, their obsession with biting or whatever weird shit is at play," she said, a faint smirk tugging at her lips for a brief second before sobering again. "But connection—real connection—is never just biology. It's built with choices."

"But what if I didn't get to make those choices? He claimed me in front of everyone without even asking."

"To save your life," she pointed out.

Rudely.

I sank lower into the water, letting the heat slap

against my skin as if it could dissolve the tension knotted beneath the surface.

"But now what? What happens if I can't live up to whatever this bond is supposed to mean to him? What happens if this all blows up in my face?" My voice broke slightly on the tail end of the question, the jagged strength of my doubts cutting through what little calm I could scrape together.

Selene arched a single brow, looking entirely unfazed by the outburst. "What happens if it doesn't?" she countered, her tone so maddeningly even it was like she knew how that question would twist inside me.

I opened my mouth only for nothing coherent to come out. I wanted to shout back, insist she hadn't seen Rath, hadn't felt the intensity he carried everywhere with him, hadn't been dragged into the gravitational pull of someone so certain of every step he took that it felt impossible to diverge.

But she just waited, her dark eyes pinning me in place the way only she could.

"It's *so* much," I finally managed, the words weak as they left me. It didn't feel like the truth, at least not the whole of it, but it was the best I could offer. "What if I want time to figure this out first? What if I need time that he can't give me?"

Selene's exhale came soft, gentle with under-standing. "Then that's what you tell him. Look, your guy strikes me as this ... overwhelming force of nature. But from what I've seen, he'd rather burn himself alive than force you into something you truly don't want. Unless it's to save your life. In which case, well, we've seen how that goes."

I gave her a flat look. "And what makes you think he'll understand? Have you *seen* how Drakarn handle emotions? Intensity is kind of their whole thing."

Selene shrugged like I'd just asked her something as simple as where she'd stashed the med kits. "They're intense. But they're not incapable of listen-ing. Remember, you're not the only one in this bond thing. If Rath values you—and clearly he does—then make him hear you. Let him understand the space you need. Building something real doesn't mean submitting to his every whim."

I let her words sit between us, their weight shifting something delicate inside me. My jaw clenched, the burning pull of doubt still smoldering, but she wasn't wrong. Rath wasn't just claiming me in the way the Drakarn did; he was offering some-thing at the core of himself, messy and complicated and raw.

The real question might not have been about Rath and his expectations but about *me*. What part of me was afraid of saying yes—because saying yes meant staying, meant stripping away every excuse I had to leave behind difficult emotions and impossible bonds I hadn't planned for.

"You're thinking," Selene murmured. "Stop trying to solve him like he's a damn equation. You can't science your way through this one, Orla."

That pulled a snort from me, my lips tugging into the first faint smile I'd felt all morning. "Are you seriously accusing me of being too logical?"

"Damn right I am." Her grin was irreverent, but her voice softened beneath it. "Listen, science girl, there's nothing logical about falling for someone—human, Drakarn, whatever. You don't get to control it, but you do get to decide what you'll do with it. So yeah, maybe you're scared. That makes sense—this is wild. But maybe lean into it a little. Give it a chance to prove itself before you shut the door completely."

A spark of laughter slipped out before I could stop it, the sound catching on the edges of my frayed emotions. "Are you sure you're qualified to play relationship guru?"

"Touché," Selene replied, unfazed. "But for what it's worth, if I had a ridiculously hot, ridiculously devoted alien hanging on my every word, I wouldn't be sitting here overthinking it. Enjoy the ride. And I do mean that literally. Figure the rest out later."

The exaggerated waggle of her eyebrows brought a laugh out of me so unexpectedly I almost startled myself with it. I shook my head as warmth unconnected to the water spread through my chest.

"Thanks. Seriously." I tilted my head back toward the slick volcanic rock, exhaling fully for what felt like the first time in hours.

"No problem." Selene leaned back in turn, her grin softening. "And hey, if you need me to punch him, you know where to find me."

"Pretty sure that'd be the shortest fight in history," I teased, finally letting the tension lose its grip on my chest entirely.

Selene kicked water at me in retaliation, and soon laughter filled the small alcove, turning the soothing peace of the baths into something warmer, something ... human.

Exactly what I needed.

THIRTEEN
ORLA

In Rath's quarters again, the silence felt heavier than it should have. I sat on the edge of the bed, my hands curled into the fabric of my pants, twisting relentlessly as I tried to find the right words. They stayed lodged in my throat.

I'd spent hours in the baths, piecing together the fragments of whatever this was—the bond, the uncertainty, the unfamiliar intensity tying me to Rath. Selene had reminded me that none of it had to make perfect sense. But that didn't mean I was any closer to understanding what I should do next.

What if I said the wrong thing? What if I couldn't give him what he was asking for? What if I fucked this whole thing up?

The door opened, and I startled, my pulse

jumping as Rath stepped into the room. His wings filled the entryway like they had every right to bend the space around them. He wasn't wearing his formal armor, just a simple combat tunic that hung unbuttoned at the throat. The red of his scales seemed sharper against the black fabric, his markings glinting faintly.

His eyes snapped to mine instantly, narrowing slightly—not in anger but in that way he always had, like he was trying to gauge every nuance of what I wasn't saying aloud. The door shut behind him, plunging us into an oppressive, expectant silence that made my chest tighten.

"You're back." His voice was low and rough, laced with something unreadable.

I nodded, swallowing hard. "I just needed to think."

Rath inclined his head, though there was a faint edge of tension in his wings—tightened, folded close. "And?"

My hands clenched tighter. "I don't know," I admitted, my voice cracking faintly. "I don't know what I'm supposed to do with ... this." I gestured vaguely at the space between us, the air thick enough to feel tangible. "With you. With ... us."

Rath's jaw tightened, but he stayed eerily still,

watching me the way a predator watches prey—not to intimidate, but to understand. To wait until my guard dropped enough for him to move.

"I—" I started and stopped, warring with the hurricane of words swirling in my chest. Finally, I just forced them out. "I don't want to ruin this. Or hurt you. I don't know what you expect—"

"There is no expectation," he said quietly, though the weight of his voice made it sound like a promise. "Not from me. Not from the bond. Only what we choose to give each other."

I stared at him, caught off guard by his directness. When I didn't respond right away, Rath stepped closer—not looming or pressing but moving into my orbit with deliberate care. His tail dragged faintly along the floor behind him, its slow sway at odds with the stillness of his shoulders and wings.

"I want to take you somewhere," he said, his gaze holding mine. "Will you come with me?"

The abrupt shift threw me, but the steadiness in his voice left me with few options for protest. My body moved almost involuntarily, standing before my mind could catch up to what I was agreeing to.

"Where?" I managed, trying to shake off the lingering nerves tightening my spine.

"You'll see," Rath replied, a faint curve brushing

the corners of his mouth. This wasn't his usual sharp edge—it was something lighter, easier. The fleeting glimpse of it eased the tension in my chest just enough for me to exhale.

Without waiting for further hesitation, Rath extended his arm. I glanced at it, then back at him. His expression didn't change, but there was something faint and vulnerable in the way he waited. Like stepping back might hurt him more than I realized.

I placed my hand lightly against his arm. Rath's claws flexed against his side, his throat dipping with a slow swallow, and then he turned, leading me wordlessly to the chamber's exit.

The walk was short, the corridors of Scalvaris familiar now, though they always seemed different when he was near—charged by his presence, by the awareness that I could always feel subtly pulling between us like gravity.

When we reached the shaft that led out toward the surface, I hesitated. It wasn't dread or fear exactly—just the unfinished idea of stepping beyond my new normal into something entirely unknown, again.

Rath stopped with me, glancing back, his head tilting just enough to catch me in his unwavering gaze. "Do you trust me?" he asked, as blunt as ever.

The question caught me sideways, throwing me off balance before I managed a simple nod.

"Hold tight," he said, and before I could ask what he meant, he swept me into his arms with effortless strength.

The air shifted sharply as his wings unfurled, the rush of volcanic wind cutting through the cavern's stale heat. Rath crouched briefly, his tail curling behind him for balance, before leaping into the vertical shaft.

I locked my arms around his neck, reflexive fear sparking in my chest, but it evaporated almost immediately. There was no faltering in his movement, no hitch of uncertainty as his wings beat powerfully against the currents, carrying us upward.

We broke through to the surface in a rush of light and heat, twin suns blazing against the horizon, their fiery glow drenching everything in gold and crimson. My breath caught as Rath gained altitude, the molten-red deserts stretching endlessly below, interrupted only by jagged peaks that sparkled like captured lightning.

The view was staggering, beautiful in a way that felt almost violent. I couldn't look away.

Rath angled his wings wide, leveling us into a smooth glide. The two suns cast long shadows against his scales, their reddish glow sharpening the dark tiger stripes that cut across his ruby red skin.

"You never see the sky like this underground, not even from the sky shafts," I said softly, more to myself than to him.

Rath's voice rumbled low, almost thoughtful. "The surface is harsher. Less forgiving. But even here, beauty survives."

I turned my head slightly against his chest, catching the faint shift in his profile as he adjusted for whatever destination we were headed toward. "Where are we going?"

"You'll see," he said simply, the words so heavy with quiet finality they felt like a vow.

It wasn't an answer. But I didn't press him. I watched the alien landscape shift below us—the streams of lava glinting like veins beneath the crust and the peaks that caught fire in the suns' light.

After what felt like an eternity wrapped in wind and alien light, Rath began to descend, his wings pulling inward as we spiraled toward a break in the terrain I hadn't noticed before. Nestled between spires of heat-resistant flora, an oasis shimmered below—a natural spring enclosed by rock walls streaked with veins of crystal. The pool radiated faint steam, kissed by the twin suns but seemingly untouched by the harshness of Volcaryth.

The sight stole my breath. It was like stepping into a memory of Earth, somehow blooming alive on a world that should have crushed it.

Rath landed gracefully at the edge of the spring. As his feet touched the ground with a solid thud, his arms remained steady, still holding me securely against him. For a moment, I clung to him, my gaze caught between the shimmering spring and the sharp edges of the cliff walls framing it. The contrast of molten hues and soft greens was surreal. The terrain around us was harsh and jagged, yet this place seemed untouched, almost sacred.

"You can let go now," Rath murmured, his voice low and impossibly soft near my ear, cutting through the reverent quiet around us.

I flushed, realizing how tightly I'd been holding onto him, and awkwardly pushed against his chest. He lowered me to the ground slowly, scanning my face for something I couldn't name before finally stepping back. His absence left a sudden, oddly cool space at my side, though his heat still lingered faintly in the air.

I turned in a slow circle, taking in the spring. The water shimmered unnaturally, its surface tinted with soft, iridescent hues—brilliant greens, blues, and purples playing against the sunlight streaming through the crystal-lined walls. Heat seeped up from the stones beneath my feet, and strange flowering plants clung to the crevices, their petals pulsing faintly as though they were alive.

"It's beautiful," I breathed.

Rath's gaze didn't leave me, though he inclined his head slightly in acknowledgment. "Few from Scalvaris come here anymore. It lies far from the usual paths, difficult to find without knowing where to look."

My chest tightened at his words. This was something special to him, something shared just with me. "So why bring me here?"

He didn't answer immediately. Instead, he turned and gestured to one of the rock formations nearby. Nestled against the spring's edge, partially hidden by heat-resistant foliage, was a small structure made of organic material—simply designed but clearly well maintained.

"It's a resting place for travelers," Rath said finally. "Warriors, scholars—any who dare to venture far from their clans, their worlds. I thought you might like to see it."

Rath's hands brushed over the markings carved

into the stone near the spring, his claws gentle against the ancient etchings. "This was built long ago, after the fall of the old world but before we founded our cities." His tone dipped slightly, tinged with something unreadable. "It was not meant for claiming territory or power. It was meant to be a place of peace."

I stared at him, the magnitude of his words settling heavily in my chest. "Then why did you bring me here?" I asked again.

He turned to face me fully. His wings shifted behind him, a restless motion that betrayed the otherwise controlled expression on his face. He stood for a moment, saying nothing, and then reached into a pouch he had strapped to his side. When his hand reappeared, he held something small but unmistakable—a dagger.

He stepped closer, holding it out between us. "This," he said, his voice low but powerful, "is for you."

The weapon was stunning. The blade itself gleamed, infused with streaks of the heat crystals I'd seen all around Scalvaris. But its hilt was something else entirely, forged from curved fragments of metal that looked unmistakably human. It must have been recovered from the crashed ship. The two materials were woven together as though they had always belonged as one.

I hesitated to reach for it. "You ... made this?"

"It was not an easy thing to create," Rath admitted. "But for you, it felt ... right."

My mouth went dry. I glanced from the dagger to his face but found no mockery or humor there—only raw, steady emotion reflected in the sharpness of his features. He extended it closer, waiting, unbending in his patience until I reached forward and accepted the weapon.

The weight of it was perfect, the hilt cool beneath my fingers while the blade seemed to hum faintly with residual warmth. I traced a finger lightly along the carved grooves of the handle, my breath catching as I realized what it represented.

"You did this to—" I faltered, struggling to find words that could encompass the enormity of the gesture. "You didn't have to do this."

"I did." Rath's voice was a low rumble, his jaw tightening faintly. "We are ... different, *shyrarva*. Orla. Of two worlds that should never have crossed. But for all our differences, the bond does not lie. You are mine, and I—" He faltered, his claws flexing at his sides before cutting through the hesitation. "I am yours. All that I have—all that I am."

The intensity of his confession pulled at something deep within me, a knot of emotion I hadn't allowed myself to untangle since this all began. I stared at him, my chest tight, the dagger trembling slightly in my grip.

He'd put everything on the table, flayed himself open before me without shame or regret.

I dropped the dagger gently onto the carved stone behind me and crossed the short space between us in two steps. Rath stiffened slightly, caught off guard, but I didn't give him time to recover. I reached up, my hands finding the planes of his face.

And then I kissed him.

Her clothes fell away like ash from a cooling forge. My claws hovered over the fastenings of her tunic, pulled back to their narrowest points as I worked the stubborn closures. A bead of sweat slid down my spinal ridge—not from heat, but from the excruciating care required not to shred the fragile human flesh.

My talons trembled as they skimmed her collarbone, her breath hitching when the blunted tips caught the strap of her breastband.

Fragile. So fragile.

The garment slithered free. Her breasts rose with her next indrawn breath, rosy peaks tightening under air that suddenly felt too thick. Two emotions warred—the urge to mark and the need to worship.

My tongue swept over an ivory-sharp fang, restraining myself against instinct's surge.

Slow.

Orla's fingers grazed my flank with agonizing hesitation, undoing the seals along my combat harness. Her blunt nails caught on an old scar near my hip. My cock throbbed at the sensation, scales flushing hotter where her knuckles brushed them. When the last clasp released, the harness fell with a heavy thud. She didn't flinch.

Her palm met the center of my chest, halting me.

"Let me," she whispered.

Her shirt followed mine to the ground. Moonlight through the steam painted her human curves in silver—soft where I was ridged, vulnerable where I was armored, perfect in all the ways that infuriated and entranced. I traced the line of Cygnus's path along her forearm with a single claw, watching goosebumps flare in its wake. The stars etched into her skin called to me, a language I couldn't parse but desperately wished to claim.

My tongue followed where my talon had traveled.

She shuddered.

Her skin tasted of salt and wild energy, humming with the same charge that gathered before a lightning storm. My lips closed around the faded ink of Ursa Major, suckling the scar tissue beneath with just enough pressure to make her fingers knot in my hair. The groan that tore from me vibrated against her pulse point—a sound I hadn't meant to release, raw and stripped of dignity.

Weakness. Sacred weakness.

Her hands found hair, not gripping but cradling. The contact speared through me—a Drakarn's head in human hands, our most guarded vulnerability. I froze, torn between wrenching away and leaning into the blasphemous intimacy.

Air hissed through my teeth.

"Look at me," she urged.

Reluctance burned like swallowed embers as I lifted my gaze. Her irises held flecks of gold now, mirrored fragments of my own eyes caught in the territory of hers. The world narrowed to that impossible symmetry.

My claws flexed against her hips.

"If I hurt you—"

"You won't."

Her certainty destroyed me.

My tongue mapped her—every constellation, every scar—laving slow, wet stripes across the faded ink of Ursa Minor. Her flesh quivered beneath the broad, flat strokes, each deliberate swipe calculated to draw gasps. When I reached Lyra's curve, I let the tip flick outward, rasping over the sensitive dip between rib and hip. Her hips jerked.

"Fuck—!"

The human curse shattered against the hut's walls as I pressed deeper, the full length of my tongue undulating now—a hot, living blade writing devotion across her abdomen. Drakarn anatomy allowed for precision no human mouth could match —broad enough to span her entire navel, pointed enough to circle a single tightening nipple.

Dragging the tip up her sternum, I paused at the scar above her heart—the one she'd inked over with dots of Andromeda. Here, my tongue softened. Broad, flat laps interspersed with the delicate pierce of its pointed end, tracing every link in the tattooed shackles until her moans turned fractured.

Her hands fisted against my ribs when I reached her throat. "Rath—!"

A warning. A plea.

I consumed both.

My tongue delved into the hollow beneath her jaw, twin points massaging the frantic pulse there. Her back arched violently, breasts brushing my scales as I worked higher—flicking her earlobe, then retreating to swirl around the shell. The vibration of her gasp traveled straight to my throbbing cock.

"You taste ...," my growl hitched as her nails found the gaps between my back plates, "like lightning."

Her thighs framed my face as I knelt—an offering and a conquest. Heat curled around us as my tongue extended to its full length to trace a path up her inner thigh. She gasped, heels digging into the notched scars between my shoulder blades. The musk of her arousal cut through the mineral air, igniting glands beneath my tongue I hadn't known could *burn*.

"Fates' breath—"

Her curse dissolved into a moan as the primary ridge of my tongue pressed against her cleft. I stilled, savoring the shiver that racked her body—the way her human softness yielded to my heat.

There.

Her hips jerked, but my tail coiled tighter around her waist—an unyielding anchor. The tip found her lower back, vibrating faintly with the rhythm of my pulse. Every gasp, every twitch of her abdominal muscles mapped directly to the swollen ridges along my cock. Pre-cum slicked the scaled base where it strained against my stomach, the tongue-like foreskin writhing against empty air.

"Look down," I growled against her thigh. "Watch what you do to me."

Her fingers tightened in my hair as she obeyed. The breath left her in a rush.

My cock arched upward—thick, veined, and glistening—the barbell piercing catching the light. The fleshy lip at its crown undulated hungrily, dripping translucent fluid that steamed where it struck the rocks.

"Rath, I—"

My tongue plunged into her without warning, the tapered tip curling upward to stroke that spongy ridge inside that I'd learned drove her mad. Her scream fractured against the walls as my fingers carefully stroked her clit. The dual assault left her thrashing—a wild thing caught in the jaws of something ancient and ravenous.

My claws found her hips, blunt tips dimpling flesh as I dragged her closer. "Come," I commanded against her quivering skin. "Mark my face with it."

Her orgasm hit like lava erupting through bedrock—a flood that drenched my chin. I drank it greedily, glands beneath my tongue swelling to absorb her essence. The taste *changed* as she peaked

—sweetness giving way to something metallic and vital, a flavor that seared itself into my marrow.

Mine.

My cock lashed the air, desperate and slick, as I rose on trembling knees. Her dazed eyes tracked the movement, lips parting as I gripped the base, smearing her release across the weeping crown.

"This," I snarled, guiding that writhing lip to her tender inner thigh, "needs you."

"Stop teasing," she gasped, nails scoring my flank.

A feral grin split my face. "Beg properly."

"Please fuck me. *Now.*"

Her plea hung in the air, and something deep in me surged to meet it. My talons flexed against her hips, the blunt tips pressing just enough to leave faint marks—not to hurt, but to claim. Her breath hitched, her body arching toward mine, and I knew I was lost.

I guided her down onto the soft moss that lined the ground, her back pressing into the warm surface as I positioned myself above her. My wings mantled around us, creating a cocoon of heat and privacy, the membrane catching the faint light filtering around us. Her eyes locked onto mine, wide and trusting, and seeing her like this—open, vulnerable, and utterly mine—sent a shudder through my scales.

"*Karys'veth ir,*" I growled, the endearment slipping from my lips as I bent to kiss her. My tongue swept against hers, hot and demanding, and she moaned into the kiss, her hands sliding up my back to grip the ridges along my spine. The sensation of her blunt nails scraping those sensitive grooves made me shudder, a low, involuntary sound rumbling from my chest.

I broke the kiss, my breath ragged, and trailed my lips down her throat, nipping lightly at the sensitive skin. Her pulse fluttered beneath my tongue, and I couldn't resist marking her there, just once, with the faintest graze of my fangs. She gasped, her hips lifting instinctively, and I growled in approval, my cock throbbing against her thigh.

"You're mine," I murmured against her skin, the words a vow and a warning. "Every part of you."

Her response was a breathless whimper as I positioned myself at her entrance, the tip of my cock pressing against her slick heat. The fleshy lip at the crown undulated eagerly, leaving a glistening trail of pre-cum as I pushed forward, inch by agonizing inch. Her body stretched to accommodate me, the sensation of her tight warmth enveloping me almost too much to bear.

"Rath—" Her voice broke on my name, her nails digging into my back as I seated myself fully inside her. I stilled, giving her a moment to adjust, my breath coming in harsh pants as I fought for control. The urge to move, to claim her completely, was a fire in my veins, but I held back, my claws flexing against her hips.

"Look at me," I commanded, my voice rough with need. Her eyes fluttered open, meeting mine, and the trust I saw there nearly undid me. I began to move, slow and deliberate, each thrust drawing a gasp or moan from her lips. The ridges along my cock dragged against her inner walls, the barbell piercing adding an extra layer of sensation that made her writhe beneath me.

Her hands slid down to grip my forearms, her nails leaving faint marks in my scales as I increased the pace. My wings tightened around us, the membrane vibrating with the force of my thrusts, and I could feel her body tightening around me, her climax building with each movement.

"Come for me," I growled, my voice a low rumble that seemed to vibrate through her. Her back arched, a cry tearing from her throat as her orgasm hit, her inner walls clenching around me in waves. The sensation was too much, and with a roar, I followed her over the edge, my release pulsing deep inside her, the scaled base of my cock throbbing with each spurt.

I collapsed onto my forearms, my breath coming in harsh gasps as I pressed my forehead to hers. Her hands slid up to cradle my face, her thumbs brushing against the scales along my jaw, and I felt something in me shift—something deep and un-nameable.

"*Karys'veth ir,*" I whispered again, the words softer this time, reverent. Her lips curved into a faint smile, and she pulled me down for a kiss, slow and tender, her body still trembling beneath mine.

The world narrowed to the rhythm of her breathing, the faint rise and fall of her chest beneath my palm. My tongue traced the curve of her shoulder, lapping at the residual slickness of our joining. The taste of her—sweet and *mine*, tinged with the smoky musk of my release—was intoxicating. My glands swelled beneath my tongue, absorbing her essence, marking her as mine in a way no Drakarn could deny.

Her fingers carded through the ridges along my spine, the touch sending shivers through my scales. I nearly purred, and she laughed softly, the vibration of it humming against my chest.

"You're trembling," she murmured, her voice still thick with the remnants of pleasure.

I lifted my head to meet her gaze, my eyes narrowing slightly. "Drakarn do not tremble," I said, though the faint quiver in my wings betrayed the lie.

Her lips curved into a knowing smile, and she reached up to brush a strand of hair from my face. The motion was so tender, so human, that it made my chest ache. My tail, still coiled loosely around her waist, tightened reflexively, pulling her closer.

"You're beautiful," she said, her voice soft but unwavering.

The words struck me like a blow, leaving me momentarily speechless. Drakarn were not beautiful—we were fierce, powerful, unyielding. But the way she looked at me, with something akin to reverence, made me feel as though I were something more.

Something worthy of her.

I leaned down to capture her lips in a slow, lingering kiss, my tongue sweeping against hers in a silent promise. When I pulled back, her eyes were half-lidded, her breath coming in shallow pants.

"I am yours," I said, the words a low rumble that vibrated through her.

Her fingers traced the line of my jaw, her touch feather-light but searing. "I know," she whispered.

I shifted slightly, my wings mantling around us as I reached for the dagger I had placed on the stone beside us. The blade gleamed in the light, the heat crystals embedded in its surface casting a soft glow. I held it out to her, the hilt resting in my palm.

"This is yours," I said, my voice rough with emotion. "A symbol of our bond. Of what could be together."

She hesitated for a moment before reaching out to take it, her fingers brushing against mine. The contact sent a jolt of heat through me, and I had to fight the urge to pull her back into my arms.

I reached out to cup her face, my claws gentle against her skin. "You are my heart's eternal flame, *shyrarva*."

Her breath hitched, and she leaned into my touch, her eyes closing briefly. When she opened them again, they were filled with a determination that made my chest swell with pride. "You keep calling me that. What does it mean?"

"It is your mating name. And I just said you are my fire's heart."

How could she not know?

Sweat had plastered some of her fading purple hair to her forehead, and she brushed it away. "And you just had that ready on the tip of your tongue when you, uh," she stumbled over the word, "claimed me?"

I could hide the full truth from her no longer.

"I'd had some time to think of it. I've known you were my mate from the moment I first laid eyes on you. Healer Mysha had to throw me out of the healing caverns when you first came to Scalvaris. I nearly tore the place apart to find you. If I had not been sent out to protect the city, I would have come for you long before that day."

My shyrarva was silent for several beats.

She placed the dagger on the stone beside us, her movements slow and deliberate. Then she reached up to pull me down into another kiss, her lips soft and demanding against mine. My wings tightened around us, shielding her from the world as I lost myself in the taste of her, in the feel of her body pressed against mine.

There was nothing else. Just her. Just us. And the bond that tied us together, unbreakable and finally whole.

FIFTEEN
ORLA

The market's chaos buzzed against my skin, every scent and shout sharpened by the low thrum of anxiety in my veins. I pressed my back against a stall draped in tapestries, their threads pulsing faintly with captured geothermal energy.

My journal lay open in my lap, half-filled with sketches of festival preparations—flame-blackened meat skewers dripping with alien spices, crystalline lanterns strung between dark pillars, a trio of Drakarn children darting underfoot with stolen sweets clutched in their claws.

I forced my pencil to keep moving, ignoring the way vendors avoided my gaze as I passed. Their slit-pupiled eyes tracked me from behind stalls, whispers hissing through sharp teeth. *Outsider. Human. False-*

mate. The words slithered around me, unspoken but unable to ignore.

With Rath, everything felt ... so freaking perfect I thought I might explode. Out here, alone, I was forced to remember everything *else.*

A familiar laugh cut through the noise. My head snapped up. *Selene.* There she was, her braid swinging as she walked beside Vega and Eden, their heads bent in conversation. Relief surged hot and sudden in my chest. I opened my mouth to call out—

They turned a corner, vanishing behind a curtain of smoldering incense.

"Damn it," I muttered, snapping the journal shut. The movement sent a flock of paperwing moths scattering from a nearby fruit cart. I stood, brushing volcanic grit from my pants, when the air shifted.

A shadow fell across my notes.

Three Drakarn warriors blocked the path, their scales dulled with ash deliberately rubbed into the grooves as if they were trying to disguise themselves. The tallest bared his fangs in a mockery of a smile. "The councilor's pet requires an escort."

No chance in hell.

My pulse spiked. "I'm fine."

The one on the left lunged.

My body moved before my mind caught up—

rock-climbing reflexes twisting me sideways, fingers scrabbling for purchase on a vendor's stall draped in gorgeous silk. The fabric wrinkled under my grip as I swung around the support beam, sending a cascade of tapestries crashing onto the warrior's head. He roared, temporarily blinded by embroidered chaos.

Sweat stung my eyes as I bolted through the gap between stalls. My boots skidded on spilled spice grains, the air thickening with the reek of singed feathers from a nearby poultry cart. A child's discarded toy nearly sent me to my knees, and I stumbled, the second warrior's claws slicing empty air where my throat had been.

"Run, little leech!" someone jeered, met with jagged laughter.

I vaulted over a crate of melons, their skins bursting under my palms. Sticky juice coated my hands as I hurled a shattered fruit at my pursuer. It exploded against his chest in a sweet spray, buying me two ragged breaths.

The third warrior materialized from the crowd's periphery, net already whirling above his head. I feinted left, then dove right toward a butcher's stall—

Too slow.

A weighted net slammed into my back like a meteor strike. Obsidian shards seared through my shirt, etching lines of fire across my shoulder blades. I hit the ground chin-first, teeth clacking together with the taste of copper. The fibers constricted with almost sentient malice, tightening with every thrash.

"Rath will flay you alive!" I snarled. My knee connected with something soft—a gratifying yelp—before four sets of claws pinned me.

"Your fire-heart's not here," the leader hissed, his breath reeking like fermented lava beetles. He pressed a talon against my windpipe, not quite breaking skin. "Scream again, and I'll gift him your vocal cords in a festival box."

A sack descended—coarse fibers soaked in Volcaryth moss extract. The world dissolved into chemical burn and muffled chaos as they dragged me across sharp gravel. I focused on the pain, mapping turns by the way shards bit into my hipbones. Left at the heated belch of bathhouse vents.

Silent tears cut through the grime on my face. Not from fear.

From fury.

"Don't worry, human," the leader purred, hauling me over his shoulder. "You'll see your mate soon."

Liar.

They dragged me through the city, but with the

bag over my head, I had no idea where we were going. Deeper, I thought. I couldn't hear the river, and it was almost overwhelmingly hot.

We finally came to a stop, and I heard the groan of metal before the Drakarn carrying me dumped me unceremoniously on my ass.

The cell door clanged shut with finality, its echo swallowed by walls weeping condensation. I pressed palms to rough volcanic stone, mapping fissures through grit-coated fingertips.

I ripped the bag off my head and took it all in.

Three paces long. Two wide. Ceiling low enough to graze my scalp if I stood straight.

Luminescent fungi smeared the walls in sickly green streaks, their light just enough to reveal the room's cruel geometry. I crouched, cheek pressed to the floor's single air vent. Sulfur and something floral tinged the stale draft.

I tested the bars, the walls, everything, hoping for some sort of weakness. I yelled for help until I was hoarse and then started again once I'd had time to recover. Hours could have passed; I had no way of knowing.

I yelled again.

"Should've gagged her properly," a guard growled beyond the door, his Drakarn consonants sharp as flint. It was too dim in the cell to get a good look at them.

His companion snorted. "Let the leech wheeze. Karyseth wants the human intact, not comfortable."

My nails bit into palms. *Karyseth.* That damned priestess who wanted me dead. This wasn't random hostility—this was politics. And revenge.

Footsteps approached. I scrambled upright, back flattening against the warmest wall—the one vibrating with geothermal currents. One of the guards came into view.

"Still breathing?" The guard's slitted eye glinted with malicious delight. "Pity."

I lunged, slamming my shoulder against reinforced metal. The impact shuddered through my bones. "Tell your coward leader to face me herself!"

Laughter rattled the door. "You're feisty for prey. We'll see if you—"

The insult dissolved into wet choking. Someone new spoke—a voice like smoldering silk. "Run along, pups. The grownups need to chat."

The guards cursed and fled.

A Drakarn I'd never seen before slouched against the frame, his emerald scales catching the fungal glow in a way that made his entire body seem to smolder with a strange green fire. Unlike Rath's warrior-straight posture, this one moved with liquid indolence, a half-eaten fruit skewer dangling from his claws.

"Well," he drawled, eyes raking over me, "you're shorter than I imagined."

I pressed harder against the rumbling wall, fingers curling around a loose stone shard. "Who the hell are you?"

He took a deliberate bite of fruit, juices running down his wrist. "Vyne. Rath's favorite nuisance." The barbell through his tongue glinted as he spoke. "He's currently two sectors away chasing false leads, thanks to Krazath's little friends. Which leaves you with me."

"Bullshit." My grip tightened on the shard. "Prove it."

Vyne sighed dramatically and reached into his tunic. My muscles coiled—until he produced Rath's mating dagger. *My* dagger. He flipped it hilt-first toward me, the blade embedding in the floor between my boots.

"He'll kill me when he finds out I touched that," he said, licking fruit residue from his claws. "His mate's blade shouldn't bear another's scent. Sentimental fool. I nicked it from your quarters before coming to find you."

I wrenched the dagger free. "If you're here to help, get me the fuck out of here."

"You *are* feisty. I see why he likes you. Unfortunately, no can do."

"What?" I surged forward, jerking the knife from the floor and pointing it at him like it would be any help with cell bars between us.

"First, I don't have the keys. The guards were scared, but they're not completely stupid. You'll be let out bright and early tomorrow for the Mating Challenge." He tossed the skewer aside.

My blade trembled in my grip. "The what?" I remembered Rath bringing it up, but I'd forgotten about that completely. And I'd certainly never agreed to it.

Vyne's tail flicked, its tip tracing idle patterns on the floor. "The Mating Challenge. It's the traditional method for weeding out weak bonds. Or disposing of political embarrassments." He leaned closer, the fungus painting his smirk toxic green. "Guess which category you're in?"

I clutched the dagger tighter. "Rath wouldn't agree to this."

"That doesn't matter." Vyne produced a vial from his belt—liquid fire swirling like captured lightning. "The Forge Temple started this; Karyseth is challenging your bond in one of the few ways that can't be denied. Either you both survive the trial tomorrow and prove yourselves, or ..." He mimed an explosion with his free hand.

"So why isn't *he* in a cell?"

Vyne rolled the vial between his claws. "He may be by now. No one's been stupid enough to volunteer for a Mating Challenge in ... a decade? Maybe more. We're all a bit rusty on the formalities. If he finds you before tomorrow, your life and his will be forfeit. But I'm not sure he cares about that right now. I've spoken to some of your friends. They say you're the smart one."

"What are you getting at?" I didn't like this man, and I couldn't trust him. What kind of friend would act this way?

"If you ever want to be accepted in Scalvaris, you need to undergo this challenge and survive. It won't satisfy Karyseth—nothing but your death will —but she's only one woman. The rest of the city will fall in line, especially with Darrokar backing you."

He sounded a lot like Terra had all those weeks ago when this all started. I really wished it was her who was talking to me.

But, damn it all, I saw his point.

My pulse hadn't stopped pounding. "How does it work?"

"Survive until sunrise. Someone will take you to the testing grounds. You and Rath face the dangers of the test—geothermal vents, shadow predators, the usual fun." He slid the vial through the bars. "One drop melts steel. Two?" His pierced tongue flicked over a fang. "Don't be nearby."

I pocketed the acid, noting how his levity didn't reach his eyes. "Why are you helping?"

"Rath's the only one who laughs at my jokes." He turned to leave, scales rippling with false nonchalance. "Oh, and human? Try not to scream when the skin sloughs off your bones. It's undignified."

Alone again, the vial settled against my thigh, its threat as volatile as my thoughts.

Did you know? I silently asked Rath's ghost. *Is this your idea of romance?*

My fingers found the dagger's hilt—Rath's craftsmanship, Vyne's theft. Both Drakarn men leaving scars in different ways. I tested the wall's weak point, volcanic grit raining down as I pried loose a handhold.

I wanted out of this cage more than almost anything else. The vial in my pocket could get me out.

But I hesitated.

The fissure taunted me—a hairline crack weeping steam near the cell's corner. I crouched before it, Vyne's vial burning a hole in my pocket. One drop could fracture the volcanic stone. Two might collapse the entire wall.

My thumb caressed the stopper.

Run.

The survival instinct drilled into me screamed for action. Melt the bars. Slip into the steam vents. Let the acidic reek of Volcaryth's underbelly cloak my escape.

I uncorked the vial.

The liquid fire hissed at exposure to air, its surface swirling with miniature plasma storms. I held it over the fissure, watching light dance across the stone. One trembling tilt would expose the weakness in the rock.

And possibly blow me to bits.

My hand froze.

Coward.

The word slithered through me in a nameless Drakarn's voice, all gravel and disappointed heat. I slammed the stopper back in place.

"Fuck you," I whispered to the phantom judgment.

But the truth coiled tighter than Vyne's acid—escaping wouldn't stop the challenge. It would only prove every sneering Drakarn right.

Human. Weak.

Unworthy.

I retreated, back pressed against the far wall. The dagger's hilt bit into my side as I methodically braided my hair—tight, practical, battle-ready. Every tug of the purple strands filled me with resolve.

Survive until sunrise.

The geothermal hum beneath my shoulders carried whispers of the arena. Vyne's casual horrors —shadow predators, flesh-melting vents—took shape in the condensation dripping down the walls. I imagined hypotheticals, calculating thermal blind spots, drafting escape vectors from half-remembered schematics of Scalvaris' underlevels.

A rasp of claws against stone snapped my head up.

"Final meal, leech."

A guard slid a clay bowl through the slot—lukewarm gruel swimming with unidentifiable protein chunks. My stomach revolted. I ate it anyway, trying to remember those honey fritters Rath had brought me.

Vyne's acid vial went into my left boot. Rath's dagger claimed a spot in the right.

The cell's oppressive heat thickened as night deepened. Sweat glued my tunic to my skin. I counted breaths, trying to meditate.

Three hundred twelve ... three hundred thirteen ...

Eventually, I must have slept.

Metal shrieked.

I jolted upright as the cell door groaned open, revealing silhouettes backlit by blood-orange torchlight.

"The challenge begins when the horn bellows." The guard's smirk dripped venom as shackles snapped around my wrists. "Hope you die quickly."

Somewhere beyond the labyrinth of stone, Rath would be hunting.

And I'd be the prey.

SIXTEEN
RATH

Orla's fear lingered in the market's choked air like smoke. Vendors scattered as I stormed through the lower districts, my scales burning so violently they cast crimson shadows across the stalls.

"Where is she?" I snarled, slamming a merchant against his own spice cart. Cinnamon pods rained down around us, their sweetness clashing with the ozone stink pouring from my overheating glands. The Drakarn's yellowish scales grayed at the edges, fear souring his scent.

"I-I swear, my lord, I saw nothing—"

My claws dug into his tunic, singeing the fabric. "Liar." The word came out a growl, my fangs inches from his throat. "Her trail ends here. Who took her? *Krazath's rats? Karyseth's zealots?*"

A child's whimper cut through the tension. I released the merchant, his wares scattering as he fled. The market's usual riot of noise had died to a hush, stall owners barricading themselves behind crates, mothers yanking fledglings into alleyways. Even the river algae's faint glow seemed dimmer, like the city itself feared my wrath.

I followed the fractured traces of Orla's scent—honeyed panic undercut by an acid tang. My wings twitched, half-unfurled, as I stalked past a butcher's stall. The proprietor froze, cleaver hovering above a lava eel's thrashing body.

"You." I gripped his arm, ignoring the eel's blood dripping down my wrist. "A human. Dragged through here. *Where?*"

The Drakarn's throat worked soundlessly before he managed, "I don't know! They went east."

I was already moving, boots crushing discarded fruit as I sprinted toward the district's eastern edge. The tunnels loomed ahead, their jagged mouths spewing geothermal steam. Orla's scent spiked here—sharp, human sweat cutting through Volcaryth's mineral reek.

Too clean.

I skidded to a halt, nostrils flaring. The trail

vanished at a rusted grate, its bars smeared with fresh blood. *Human* blood. My vision hazed red.

My claws found purchase in the grate's hinges, muscles straining as I wrenched it open. Metal screamed, the sound swallowed by the chasm below.

Empty.

No body. No scent. Just a scrap of fabric caught on a rust spike—purple, like the strands she dyed in her hair. I crushed it in my fist, the growl building in my chest shaking the walls.

They'd scrubbed her. Stolen her. *Dared.*

A guard approached, spear trembling in his grip. "Blade Councilor, the protocols demand—"

I backhanded the weapon into the abyss, my claws leaving gashes in his shoulder plates. "Demand *this*," I spat, storming past him. "Find her. Or burn."

I couldn't blindly follow her trail, not when it disappeared. I picked up my pace, heading for a place that might have answers.

The council chambers' doors loomed ahead when *his* stench hit me—rotten sulfur and ambition. Krazath stepped from a side passage, wings tucked in a mockery of deference, his scales dulled by ash.

"Looking for something, my lord?" His tongue flicked over the fresh scar on his throat—the one *I'd* given him days prior.

I didn't slow. "Move."

He sidestepped, tail lashing. "Or what? You'll burn another market down?" His laughter echoed off the corridor's crystalline veins. "Pathetic. The great Rath brought low by—"

My claws sank into his throat before he finished. I slammed him against the wall, fissures spiderwebbing through volcanic stone. His pupils blew wide, but the smirk stayed.

"Where. Is. She." Spittle hissed against his scales.

Krazath's gills flared, struggling to draw air. "Already in the Pit," he choked. "By dawn, the shadows will peel her soft human flesh while she screams your name. A fitting end for a false mate."

The wall cracked deeper under his skull. Krazath's bravado wavered as heat warped the air between us.

"Kill me," he rasped, "and your human dies slower. The challenge demands *both* participants."

My grip loosened.

He wheezed a laugh, blood flecking his teeth. "The priestess invoked the ancient rites—no bond, no trial. If you're not in the arena at sunrise, they'll feed her to the beasts piece by piece."

I dropped him. He crumpled, gasping, but still sneering.

Krazath's taunts chased me down the corridor—a jagged sound cut short by the click of claws on stone. Zarvash emerged from the council chamber's shadowed archway, flanked by two scribes clutching slates.

"Rash actions won't reclaim your mate," he said. One scribe stepped forward, offering a slate displaying legal script. I smashed it against the wall, shattering the screen into glittering shards.

Zarvash didn't flinch. "The challenge is a mercy. Would you prefer Karyseth's alternative? A public execution by molten immersion?"

One of the scribes shifted, revealing Orla's journal clutched in his claws. My vision tunneled.

"Give. That. To me."

I lunged.

Mektar seemed to materialize from nothingness —a midnight-blue blur—his tail snapping around my throat. Scales bit into my windpipe as he wrenched me backward. My claws scraped stone, leaving furrows in the floor.

"Cease," Mektar hissed, the first word I'd heard him speak in weeks. His spiked tail tightened, forcing me to my knees.

Zarvash plucked the journal from the scribe's grip, flipping through pages filled with Orla's cramped sketches and notes. "Fascinating. She documented our geothermal vents' resonance frequencies. Clever for a primitive."

"Primitive?" I choked out. "She survived all this world has thrown at her."

"Barely."

"She never agreed to this challenge, nor did I," I snarled.

Zarvash shrugged. "Irrelevant. It proceeds at dawn. Fight beside her, and you might both survive. Fight me now," he leaned down, copper eyes reflecting my twisted expression, "and she dies screaming, alone."

Mektar's tail loosened just enough to let me breathe.

"Choose, Flame Heart," Zarvash murmured. "Warrior or fool."

Darrokar appeared in the archway, Nyx at his flank like a steel-scaled shadow. The Warrior Lord's obsidian scales pulsed with restrained energy, his gaze sweeping over my battered state. "Stand down, Rath."

Mektar let me go. He and Zarvash made their escape.

I whirled. "You knew."

Darrokar sidestepped, blocking the entrance with his bulk. "I didn't sanction this."

"Liar!" The word erupted in a shower of sparks from my overheating glands. "Someone on the council had to. You let them drag her into their sick ritual!"

Nyx shifted, his steel-gray scales rasping like drawn blades. "You don't think that councilor just ran out of this room like his scales were on fire? Zarvash is a snake. But the challenge is older than the city; it can't be avoided now that it's begun. You know this."

I rounded on Darrokar, my wings flaring wide enough to brush the corridor's crystal veins. "I don't see you volunteering to prove your bond with a human."

Darrokar's claws flexed, the only betrayal of his anger. "Terra earned her place through combat. You have done nothing to win over the doubters but hide away with your mate as if she's a shameful secret."

The accusation struck like a lava whip. My fist connected with his jaw before I'd fully decided to swing. The crack echoed through the cavern—bone meeting scale, blood meeting fire.

Darrokar staggered, blood welling from a split

lip. Nyx moved between us in a blur, his tail slamming into my chest hard enough to bruise. Breath exploded from my lungs as I skidded backward, claws screeching against stone.

"Enough!" Nyx roared, planting himself between us. "Kill each other after the human's safe."

Darrokar wiped his mouth, staring at the blood on his claws in disbelief. "You think I *want* this?" he snarled, advancing on me. "If Orla dies in that pit, *you* unravel. And Scalvaris needs you whole."

I spat at his feet. "Scalvaris can burn."

Nyx's tail snapped out, pinning me against the wall. "You'd abandon thousands for one?"

"Yes." The word left no room for debate. "For her. Absolutely."

Darrokar's nostrils flared, the scent of my conviction thickening the air. For a heartbeat, I saw it—the same recklessness that once made him charge a lava serpent bare-handed. Then it vanished beneath the Warrior Lord's mask.

"Dawn approaches swiftly," he said coldly. "Prepare for your human."

I laughed—a broken, sulfurous sound. "Or what? You'll lock me in a cell too?"

Nyx's tail withdrew. I shoved past him, my claws leaving fresh gouges in the council chamber's doorframe. Darrokar's voice haunted me as I walked away—a growl laced with something that might've been regret. I didn't look back.

The city blurred around me. Drakarn fled into side tunnels as I stormed toward the training grounds, my wings scraping the floor.

The caverns loomed ahead, their arched entrance carved with reliefs of ancient warriors. I remembered the first time I'd walked these halls as a fledgling—pride swelling as my mother's claws rested on my shoulder. Now, the stone faces seemed to sneer.

I seized the nearest combat dummy, its straw guts spilling as I hurled it into a rack of lava-forged spears. Metal clattered like bones. My tail lashed out, shearing through a target post. Splinters rained down, mixing with the acrid stench of my over-heating scales.

"False mate!" The dummy's head came off in my hands, its painted eyes mocking. I crushed it to pulp.

A rack of training swords collapsed under a wing strike, blades scattering like teeth. One skittered toward the arena's edge, its hilt catching the faint glow of heat crystals. I stomped it into the gravel, the snap of volcanic steel echoing through the cavern.

"Weakling!" Another dummy met my claws, its torso ribbons fluttering to the bloodstained sand.

Memories surged—Orla's kiss after I'd wiped the floor with the *kervash* I now couldn't kill. I could still taste her on my tongue. Human. Fragile.

Mine.

The last dummy exploded in a shower of splinters. I stood heaving in the wreckage, sulfurous breath fogging the air. Across the arena, my reflection warped in a polished obsidian shield—a crimson-scaled monster haloed by destruction.

I ripped the shield from the wall and hurled it. The crash reverberated around me.

"Had enough?"

Darrokar's voice.

I didn't turn. "Walk away before I do something we'll both regret."

Silence. Then retreating footsteps.

Alone, I sank to my knees, claws buried in sand still damp from yesterday's training bouts. The vents above hissed, their steam carrying the distant roar of the sacred river. Somewhere beneath that sound, Orla waited.

I pressed my forehead to the ground, inhaling the mineral tang of Scalvaris's heart. Her face burned behind my eyelids—not afraid. Never afraid. Defiant. Clever. *Alive.*

When I rose, the training ground's eastern wall bore fresh scars.

"If the city wants a challenge, I'll give them a war."

SEVENTEEN

ORLA

I barely had time to lurch upright before the guards' claws closed around my arms, dragging me into an opening so violently orange it seared my retinas. My boots skidded across sand still steaming from whatever butchery had occurred here last, and with each step, the heat rose in waves that curled the edges of my vision.

The arena hit me in layers—acrid sweat thick enough to coat my tongue, sulfurous vents belching toxic fumes, the metallic tang of old blood baked into volcanic stone until it reeked like rust and rot.

Cheers erupted from tiered seating writhing with Drakarn spectators, each pair of eyes reflecting a savage hunger. My knees nearly buckled at the sight of them, but the guards jerked me upright, their laughter vibrating through my bones, a cruel counterpoint to the crowd's thunderous roars.

And there, in one tiny section, were my fellow humans. Selene, Eden, Kaiya, Vega, Kira, Lexa, Hawk, Rachel, and on the end was Terra, standing next to her hulking Drakarn mate, Darrokar. None of them were cheering. They looked like they were watching a funeral.

Thanks for the vote of confidence, girls.

"Run fast, leech," a guard hissed, shoving me forward with a push that sent me stumbling across the scorched ground.

The gate slammed shut behind me, a boom louder than the entire crowd. I spun, heart hammering, taking stock through the adrenaline-fueled haze. Jagged pillars rose around me, their shadows crisscrossing over thin crusts of stone hiding lava's glow. To the east, a geothermal vent coughed superheated steam in irregular bursts. My fingers twitched, itching for my journal's grid paper to calculate patterns, to cling to something orderly in this bedlam.

A pebble clattered to my right.

I turned just as the ground erupted, a nightmare uncoiling from the shadows. The monster's maw yawned wide, rows of serrated teeth glowing like filaments in a furnace. Its scales weren't just black—they drank the light, a void edged with ember cracks that pulsed with each thunderous heartbeat. Steaming saliva dripped from its jaws, hissing where it struck the sand and sending up acrid plumes that seared my nostrils.

Acid spit. Great.

The crowd's roar became a distant buzz as the lava lizard's throat rattled. Its tongue lashed out, forked and flickering with actual flames, testing the air. I felt the heat of it from six feet away, a dry slap against my sweat-slicked skin. My thoughts scattered with a single directive: *Survive first. Panic later.*

It lunged.

The world blurred.

I threw myself sideways, shoulder slamming into a jagged pillar as claws the size of steak knives carved through the space where my throat had been. Hot stone tore at my shirt, branding my ribs. The lizard's momentum carried it past me, its spiked tail whipping my thigh hard enough to bruise. A thunderous impact shattered rock behind me, bits of obsidian scattering like glass shards across the steaming sand.

A second predator exploded from a fissure to my left, smaller and faster—a juvenile, maybe, its scales dull gray but eyes burning with the same unending hunger. It scuttled sideways like a crab, claws click-click-clicking on stone, herding me toward the arena's western edge. My pulse pounded in my ears; panic tried to grip my throat. I forced a shaky breath, stuffing that fear to the edges of my mind.

I risked a glance over my shoulder.

Bad move.

A third lizard dropped from a ledge above, all rippling muscle and furnace stink. It landed in a crouch, tail lashing, black claws digging grooves into the sand. This one's scales shimmered with a nauseating oil-slick sheen, and a heat mirage rose from its spine like a ghostly halo.

They fanned out, driving me backward. My heel brushed something brittle—the sand here was thinner, the stone beneath glowing faintly orange through cracks. Something lay under there, and every inch of my body screamed that I *didn't* want to find out what.

The juvenile struck first, springing with a guttural shriek. I ducked, its claws snagging my hair as I rolled. Purple strands fluttered to the sand, instantly singed in the heat. This was not good. The largest lizard charged, maw gaping, and on instinct, I dove between its legs.

Putrid heat engulfed me as I slid beneath its

belly, scales scraping my back raw. Its underbelly wasn't armored, just a leathery hide. I drove my elbow upward, aiming for a soft pocket. My bones shook with the impact.

The beast bellowed so loudly it shook stalactites. It bucked, tail slamming down where I'd been half a breath before. I scrambled upright, lungs burning from the sulfur stink.

"Come on, you overgrown gecko," I snarled, voice trembling despite the bravado tearing through my veins.

The oil-slick lizard answered by vomiting a stream of liquid fire.

I hurled myself behind a pillar. Flame splashed against stone, droplets spattering my boot. The synthetic material melted instantly, searing my ankle.

I screamed, and the crowd cheered louder.

"Not fucking today." I edged along the pillar, trying to suck in scorching air without passing out.

The nearest lizard's tail lashed out. I scrambled upward, rock-climbing instincts kicking in as I scaled the unstable column. A claw snagged my boot heel, and I kicked hard, feeling scale crunch under my foot. The lizard recoiled with a shriek, buying me two seconds to scramble up as high as I could.

From this vantage point, the arena spread below me like some demon's playground: cracked stone, churning pockets of lava, spouts of toxic steam. The crowd's jeers shifted pitch. All three lizards circled, acid drool pooling, jaws grinding in anticipation of a meal. One began scaling the pillar, its toes finding purchase in the porous stone. Others prowled below, yellow eyes glinting.

I fumbled for Vyne's vial. The acid sloshed inside, its surface shimmering like liquid rage.

One drop melts steel.

The lizard's head crested the ledge, jaws unhinging. I hurled the vial. It was my only shot, and each heartbeat pounded in my skull as though time itself slowed.

It struck between its eyes.

The explosion of sizzling flesh drowned the crowd's gasps. The lizard tumbled backward, its death throes scattering the pack. I slid down the pillar, boots skidding in gore-streaked sand. My hands shook, the adrenaline a sickening high.

There was no sign of the vial. I could yell at myself for wasting it later. If I survived.

Where the hell was Rath?

A hiss rippled through the arena—sharper, hungrier than the lizards.

I turned slowly, dread pooling in my gut. The ground beneath my boots trembled as a new shadow uncoiled from a deep tunnel, its scales clicking like a death rattle. It was like a living earthquake: pulsing, breathing, lethal.

I backpedaled, ankle screaming where melted boot leather fused to burnt flesh. The creature rising from the pit wasn't lizard—not with those segmented metallic plates rippling along its thirty-foot length, not with the dozen articulated legs tipped in hooked barbs that screeched against stone.

Its head swung toward me on a serpentine neck, faceted eyes reflecting a thousand fractured images of my trembling form. Molten veins pulsed beneath pulsing yellow scales, casting hellish light through the joints in its armor. The stench of rotting sulfur and singed bone clawed at my nostrils as it hissed, spined tail whipping behind it in arcs that carved gouges in the arena floor.

A roar split the air—not the beast's, but familiar. *Mine.*

Rath dropped from the ceiling like a comet trailing smoke, wings folding tight against his back as he landed. Twin lava-forged swords blazed in his claws, their edges white-hot as he landed between me and the monstrosity. Sand vaporized where his boots struck, the shockwave knocking me to my knees. His scales glowed with an infernal intensity, veins of orange light flickering in the cracks along his arms and shoulders.

"Stay behind me!" he barked, voice rough, scorching. I'd never been happier to be yelled at.

The wyrm struck.

Rath's swords met its jaws in a shower of sparks. I scrambled backward as acid-green blood rained down, eating pockmarks into the sand. The wyrm's barbed legs scissored wildly, shearing off chunks of Rath's armor. He didn't flinch, driving a blade upward through its palpitating throat. A gush of fluorescent ichor splattered the closest rock face, sizzling on contact.

"Orla! The pillar!"

I turned toward his shout just as a wyrmling— smaller, faster—spewed liquid fire from above. Heat slapped my shoulders, singeing the ends of my hair even worse than before. I dove behind a stalagmite, fists clenched. The stone exploded behind me in a shower of fragments, shrapnel scraping against me.

Rath's wing clipped my side as he soared past, snatching the wyrmling mid-leap. They crashed into the arena wall in a tangle of scales and snapping jaws. I didn't wait—I snatched up a fallen barb the size of my forearm, its edge still dripping wyrm blood that sizzled against my palm.

"Stubborn human!" Rath roared, pinning the wyrmling with a knee to its sparking thorax. His free sword hovered at its shuddering neck. "I said stay—"

The sand between us bulged.

We moved in together—Rath yanking his blade free, me driving my stolen barb downward. The emerging wyrm pup died with a wet gurgle, acidic blood spraying my forearms. I barely felt the new burns, adrenaline numbing everything but the will to keep fighting.

Rath's claw closed around my bicep, hauling me toward a crumbling stone column. He wrapped his arms around me, tail securing me in place, and launched us up. The ground below vanished, swirling steam and predator eyes glaring with ravenous malice.

But there was no hope of escaping the arena. We were closed in, and I didn't need to be told that the only way out was to win. Whatever winning meant to the Drakarn.

Rath carefully set me down on top of one of the pillars, obsidian shards scraping the soles of my boots. "Stay. Here." His voice thrummed with command.

"Not arguing!" I shouted back, though my pulse hammered in protest.

But there was barely any sanctuary on top of the pillar, just crumbling rock and a panoramic view of certain death. Rath's wings blotted out the arena's hellish glow as he dove back toward the writhing wyrm. I stood alone with the sizzle of my burnt flesh and the acidic reek of dead reptiles filling my lungs, the noise of the crowd rolling in thunderous waves.

Something clicked beneath me.

I looked down. The stone under my boots swam with shadows—no, not shadows. *Scales.* Dozens of them, rippling up the pillar in a shimmering wave. Snakes. Their arrowhead skulls broke the surface first, lidless eyes burning with phosphorescent hate, forked tongues tasting my terror.

I dug in my boot, heart pounding like a war drum, yanking my dagger from my boot just in time.

The first strike came from behind. I pivoted, the snake's fangs grazing my hip as I brought the blade down in a wild arc. Metal bit through scale and bone, severing a skull that rolled hissing into the abyss. Acid blood sprayed my wrist—agony, then a terrifying numbness that spread like wildfire.

They swarmed.

I became a creature of instinct—jabbing, sneering, kicking when teeth closed around my boot. A tail lashed my ribs. Another snake coiled around my thigh, its body searing like a brand. The sound of them—tangled hisses, the scrape of scales on rock—flooded my ears, drowning out the roar of the crowd for a moment.

The world tilted, and the ledge crumbled.

The pillar shuddered beneath me. The snakes' bodies coiled around the column's base, a living noose tightening as they gnawed through rock with fangs dripping corrosive venom.

The crumbling ledge offered less footing than a cliffside ice sheet. Below, a lava pit bubbled hungrily, shooting up flares of liquid rock that made the entire air shiver. Above, Rath's battle cries mingled with the wyrm's shrieks, savage echoes that slammed around the arena in waves of terror and adrenaline.

And the ledge gave way.

I caught a jagged outcrop one-handed, body slamming into the pillar's searing surface. A snake clung to my boot, its weight dragging me toward the lava's orange maw. The heat radiating from below scorched my cheeks. I tasted salt from sweat rolling down my lip.

"Not ... a chance," I snarled, swinging my free leg in a desperate arc.

The snake's skull crunched against the rock. It released me, spiraling into the lava with a hissing pop. I hauled myself onto the outcrop, trembling arms screaming with exertion. Below, the remaining snakes writhed, their acid melting handholds into treacherous sludge, and the stench of dissolving stone added a bitter tang to the suffocating air. The largest snake struck like a piston, fangs glistening with fresh venom. I twisted, driving my dagger upward, praying it would hold.

The blade glanced off its armored snout but lodged in its eye.

It recoiled, shrieking, the dagger protruding from the snake's ruined socket like a gruesome trophy. It thrashed, tail smashing the pillar and shaking the entire structure.

Rock exploded. I fell and caught the snake's spasming body.

We dropped together, its acid blood eating through my sleeve. The lava's heat blistered my cheeks, shriveled my lungs. I wrenched the dagger free as we plummeted, stabbing wildly. The blade struck a chink in its underbelly armor.

Green gore erupted, hissing in midair.

The snake's final throes flung me sideways. I hit a sloping rockface and slid, shredding my palms on volcanic stone. The lava pool yawned inches away, each bubble a promise of burning finality.

Move.

I crab-crawled upward, dagger clenched between my teeth. Rath's roar guided me—a beacon in the inferno. I launched myself the last few feet over a jagged lip of rock, vision spinning with exhaustion. I was still alive.

I crested the slope in time to see him grappling the wyrm, its metallic scales refracting hellish light. One of his swords lay shattered nearby, broken edges still glowing. The wyrm's tail coiled around his torso, squeezing the air from his lungs.

"Hey, glitterlizard!" I hefted my blade, voice raw.

The wyrm's faceted eyes pivoted.

I leaped onto its thrashing tail, driving my knife toward a gap in its plates. The impact jolted my wrist, and my grip slipped. My weapon spun away, clattering somewhere I couldn't see.

"Orla, no!" Rath bellowed, baring fangs as he tried to twist free.

The wyrm shook me off like a gnat. I rolled, snatching a shard of Rath's broken sword—still glowing white-hot. It scorched my fingers, but pain was an afterthought.

The wyrm struck.

I met its jaws with the shard.

Molten steel met crystalline fangs.

The explosion blinded me. A searing flash that devoured all sound, all light, all sense of direction. When the blaze in my retinas finally subsided, the wyrm lay twitching, its skull split by the shard wedged deep in its neural crest. Rivulets of sickly fluid seeped from the wound, burning channels into the arena floor. Rath stood over it, chest heaving, his remaining sword trembling in his grip.

Raw fury radiated off him in waves.

He stared at me, breath ragged, eyes blazing with the reflection of the crowd's cheers.

I wiped wyrm guts from my cheek. "You're welcome," I rasped, somehow finding the breath to speak.

His tail lashed, stirring up a cloud of dust and ash. "You were supposed to stay on the pillar!"

"And you were supposed to duck." I pointed to the wyrm's barb embedded in his shoulder.

The arena shuddered—a deep, groaning vibration that traveled up through my boots and into my teeth. Rath's hand closed around my wrist an instant before the ground split between us, superheated steam screaming from fresh fissures. The entire stadium pulsed with an ominous quake, as if the volcano beneath us throbbed with a living heart.

"Move!" he roared, yanking me sideways as a geyser erupted where we'd stood, white-hot droplets splattering across the stone.

Three lava-lizards crawled out of an opening near the geyser.

We crashed into the arena wall, my spine slamming against rock still hot from the wyrm's acid blood. Rath's body shielded mine as another vent burst overhead, raining scalding drops that sizzled on his scales. The crowd above howled for blood, their savage chants echoing across the ring.

Three vents formed a tightening triangle. I had an idea. "Drive the lizards into the steam."

Rath's answering snarl held reluctant approval. He lunged left, swords carving arcs that forced the three new lizards toward the nearest fissure. I scrambled up a rubble pile, torn boots slipping on loose shale. My burns screamed with every movement, but I forced my body onward.

The largest lizard wheeled toward me, jaws dripping. It leaped in a swirl of obsidian dust. I ducked and screamed, "Now!"

Rath's blade slammed into the vent's edge, diverting

the steam jet directly into the creature's face. The lizard's death throes filled the arena with an earsplitting wail that harmonized with the crowd's frenzied cheers, hunger for violence intensifying their mania.

We fell into rhythm—Rath herding, me hurling chunks of broken rock to trigger the vents. When the final lizard collapsed in a steaming heap, we stood back-to-back, shoulders heaving in sync. Blood—my own, and a nauseating medley of reptilian gore—dripped off me in rivulets.

The wyrm's corpse chose that moment to slide into a lava pit, half-submerged, releasing a final gargle.

The resulting explosion of molten rock sent us diving in unison. Rath's wing curled around me as fiery debris rained down, clanging off his scaled armor. His growl vibrated through my burned cheek, pressed against his chest. "Still alive?"

"Disappointed?" My lips cracked on the word, tasting ash and iron.

His fanged grin flashed in the flickering glow. Despite everything, a flicker of satisfaction sparked in his eyes—a warrior's thrill at survival against impossible odds.

We were alive. We won.

Do you believe in our fucking bond now? I wanted to scream into the stands.

Across the bloodied sand, Zarvash rose from the spectator stands, his bronze scales polished to a taunting gleam under the shifting torchlight. His presence commanded the crowd's attention, and the cheers fell into an eager hush.

"The Forge remains unimpressed!" he bellowed, ceremonial hammer raised high. A small section of the crowd took up the chant, dozens of claws pounding stone in rhythmic unison.

Unworthy. Unworthy. Unworthy.

The rest of the Drakarn watched in silence, tension coiling in the air like a serpent.

The ground beneath us groaned, fresh steam vents hissing open. Rath shoved me backward as a geyser erupted where I'd stood, the superheated blast singing his scales. Pain flickered across his features, a snarl following in its wake.

"Coward!" Rath roared, twin swords flaring brighter, red lines tracing the steel. "You hide while others bleed!"

Zarvash launched himself out of the stands and glided down, wings spread wide, each leathery membrane etched with golden runes. "Tradition requires *proof,* Flame Heart. Your human barely survived glorified hatchling trials." His copper-tipped tail flicked toward the smoldering wyrm carcass. "The Forge demands a true sacrifice."

I limped forward, ankle screaming like the flesh might peel away. "We just killed your murder pets. What more—"

Zarvash backhanded me with his tail. A blow so swift that I barely caught the glint of bronze scales before it connected. He was fast, impossibly so.

The world whited out. I tasted blood before feeling the split lip, my skull ringing from the impact. Rath moved faster than thought—his sword at Zarvash's throat, heat radiating off him in waves that distorted the air.

"Touch her again," Rath growled, embers dripping from his fangs, "and I'll mount your scales on my wall."

The arena held its breath as the crowd leaned forward in eager anticipation. Even the lava vents seemed to quiet momentarily, their hissing subdued beneath the tension.

Zarvash laughed—a dry, rustling sound that made my skin crawl. He pressed forward until Rath's blade drew blood. "Strike me down, and the challenge fails. It is not over until the gong chimes." His tongue flicked toward the shadowed alcove where

Karyseth's priests lurked next to a massive bronze gong, arms crossed. They made it clear the gong would not chime until one or both of us were dead.

It might have ended there, blood spilled to feed the arena's greed, but Darrokar approached with a thunderous stride, his black wings stirring the dusty air. It took little more than his furious glare for one of the priests to step aside.

Darrokar raised a scaled fist and rang the gong, the brassy note echoing across the volcanic arena like the final toll of judgment.

The challenge was over.

Rath spat at Zarvash's feet, the hiss of saliva evaporating on contact. "You are a coward and the Forge Temple's lackey. Meet me in the ring and repay this insult. *Now*."

EIGHTEEN
RATH

The arena's stench clung to me—sulfur, blood, and the acrid tang of molten rock. My scales still smoldered, the faint glow of heat lines flickering across my arms as I stormed through the training grounds' arched entrance. Orla limped beside me, her human frame trembling with exhaustion, her purple-streaked hair singed and matted with wyrm blood.

She was alive.

That was all that mattered. But the fire in her eyes told me she wasn't done fighting.

"You're insane," she said, her voice hoarse but sharp enough to cut through the haze of my rage. "We just survived that nightmare, and your first thought is to pick another fight?"

I didn't stop walking. This ended today. I would not wait another moment. "Krazath is Zarvash's underling. He wouldn't act without orders. Zarvash orchestrated your kidnapping on behalf of the temple. He put you in that pit. He doesn't get to walk away unscathed."

"And what if you lose?" she shot back, grabbing my arm with a strength that surprised me. Her fingers were small, fragile against my scales, but her grip was iron. "What happens to me then? To *us*?"

I turned, my tail lashing behind me, and met her glare. Her face was streaked with soot and blood, her lower lip split and swollen. But her eyes—those damned human eyes—burned with defiance. She wasn't afraid of me, even now. Even after everything.

Good.

"I won't lose," I growled, the words rumbling deep in my chest. "Not to him. Not ever."

She scoffed, releasing my arm and crossing hers over her chest. "You're not invincible, Rath. You're bleeding, exhausted, and—"

"And I'll tear him apart," I interrupted, my voice rising enough to echo off the cavern walls. The training grounds were empty for now, the usual clatter of weapons and shouts of sparring warriors absent. The crowd would migrate from the challenge grounds soon enough, their need for blood never sated. Even the air felt heavier, charged with anticipation for what was coming. "He threatened you. He put you in danger. That's not something I can let slide."

Orla opened her mouth to argue, but a sharp hiss of pain cut her off. She clutched her side, her face paling as she doubled over. My anger faltered, replaced by a surge of guilt. I'd been so focused on survival and ending this that I hadn't fully registered the extent of her injuries.

"Selene!" I barked, my voice carrying through the cavern to the group trailing us. The human medic appeared almost instantly, her medkit slung over one shoulder and her dark hair pulled into a tight braid. She moved with the efficiency of someone used to chaos, her sharp eyes scanning Orla's wounds.

"Sit," Selene ordered, gesturing to a nearby bench. Orla hesitated, her gaze flicking to me, but Selene wasn't having it. "Now. Unless you want to lose your damned foot."

Orla sat, wincing as Selene began cleaning the burns on her arms and legs. The medic's hands were steady, her movements precise, but Orla's jaw clenched with every touch. She didn't complain, though.

"I need to do this," I said, my voice softer now but no less adamant. "It won't stop until he feels true consequences."

Orla looked up at me, her eyes narrowing. "Killing him is quite the consequence. Isn't that just going to piss the Forge Temple off more?" She winced as Selene hit a particularly sensitive spot. "I'm not trying to stop you. I'm trying to make sure you don't get yourself killed."

"I'm not going to kill him," I said, tail lashing. "I want to. He kidnapped you. He threw you into that pit. But there are rules to this. If I don't challenge him, he'll think he can get away with it. They all will."

She held my gaze for a long moment, her expression unreadable. Then, slowly, she nodded. "Okay. But I'm not leaving. If you're going to fight him, I'm going to watch."

"You need medical attention," I argued, gesturing to Selene, who was now applying a salve to Orla's burns.

"And I'm getting it," Orla snapped. "But I'm not missing this. Not after what he did."

Selene glanced between us, her lips pressed into a thin line. "She's stubborn," she said, her tone dry. "But she's right. She's stable enough to stay. Watching *only*." Selene jabbed a finger at my mate. Then she turned to me. "You should really have a healer take a look at you before you add to your own injury list."

I growled low in my throat, torn between my need to protect Orla and my desire to make Zarvash pay. In the end, it was the fire in her eyes that decided it. She wasn't just my mate—she was my equal. And if she wanted to stand by me, I wouldn't deny her that.

"You can watch," I said, my voice rough. "But I want you sitting next to Selene."

Orla smiled, though it was strained by pain. "Deal. Now go kick his ass."

Her words sparked something in me—a fierce pride that burned hotter than any flame. I turned toward the training ground's center, where Zarvash was already waiting, his bronze scales gleaming under the faint glow of the heat crystals. His copper-highlighted tail flicked lazily, his expression one of cool amusement.

"Flame Heart," he called, his voice dripping with mockery. "Ready to bleed?"

I bared my fangs. "Ready to end this."

The crowd of Drakarn who had gathered to witness the duel stood in a loose circle, their scales glinting in the light of the heat crystals embedded in the cavern walls and coming through the sky shaft overhead. Their eyes were fixed on me and Zarvash.

I had expected more to make their way from the challenge grounds. Apparently, a simple honor duel was not worth the hike for most.

Pyroth stepped forward, his orange scales catching the light as he moved with the grace of a predator. Crimson swirls in the pattern of his scales seemed to ripple with each step, and his presence commanded the attention of everyone in the room. He was the Blade Dancer, the master of combat artistry.

"Warriors," Pyroth began, his voice deep and resonant, carrying the weight of ancient rituals. "You stand here today bound by the traditions of our people. This is not a fight to the death, but a test of skill, honor, and resolve. Let the flames guide your blades, and may the suns judge your worth."

He raised a clawed hand, and the crowd fell silent.

Zarvash smirked, his tail flicking lazily as he unsheathed his daggers. The blades were sleek and deadly, their edges honed to a razor-sharp finish. He twirled them in his claws with practiced ease, the movement fluid and mocking.

I drew my lava-forged swords, the white-hot edges glowing as I settled into a fighting stance. The weight of the blades was familiar, comforting, even if the sword in my left hand was a backup blade, my favored weapon sacrificed to the Mating Challenge.

This wasn't just about me—it was about Orla, about proving to every Drakarn in Scalvaris that she was mine to protect, and that no one—*no one*—could threaten her without consequences.

Pyroth began to chant, his voice rising and falling in the rhythm of an ancient war song. The words were older than the city itself, and they carried the history of countless battles fought and won. The crowd joined in, their voices blending as they stamped their feet in an ancient beat. The sound stirred something deep within me.

Zarvash's smirk widened. "You will lose," he taunted, his voice dripping with condescension. "You're already bleeding."

I didn't respond. Words were useless here. The only language that mattered was the clash of steel and the roar of flames. I tightened my grip on my swords, the heat from the blades searing my palms, and waited for Pyroth's signal.

The Blade Dancer raised his hand, the chant reaching its peak. The crowd fell silent, tension in the air so thick it was almost suffocating. Then, with a sharp downward motion, Pyroth gave the signal.

The duel began.

Zarvash lunged, moving faster than I expected. He closed in, daggers slashing for my neck. I parried with one sword, the collision sending sparks across the stone. The impact trembled through my arms, but I stayed rooted. I swung my second blade in a counterstrike aimed at his ribs. He twisted clear, a smug grin curling his mouth.

He circled me, wings tense at his back. His footwork was nimble, the daggers an extension of his body. My swords were heavier; I relied on power and reach, but he had speed. He tested me with a quick thrust, then darted away before I could answer. We danced around each other, eyes locked, searching for any opening.

He feinted left. I caught the shift in his stance and recognized the real strike on my right side. Metal screamed as I blocked, but he flicked his tail low, raking a spiked tip across my shin. I hissed through clenched teeth. He was trying to goad me into a rash move.

"Is this all, Flame Heart?" he mocked, voice pitched just loud enough for the crowd to hear. "I expected more from you."

I let the barb pass, keeping my breathing steady. His arrogance was a weapon I could turn against him.

He came at me again, daggers blurring in a flurry of slicing arcs. I managed to block most, but one found a gap and scored a cut along my upper arm. The burn of pain sharpened my focus. I smashed my pommel toward his face, forcing him back. He hopped away, wings flaring to maintain balance, eyes gleaming with the thrill of combat.

We circled each other once more. The watchers pressed in, hungry for blood and a show. I caught the slightest movement near the edge—Orla, standing with Selene, her posture rigid. I reminded myself she was alive, there, trusting me to handle this. That alone fueled me with savage resolve.

Zarvash attacked again, eyes narrowing. He aimed for my torso in a quick combination, then pivoted to strike at my flank. This time, I caught his left dagger with one blade, hooking his right with the other in a crunch of steel against steel. Our locked weapons screeched. I shoved forward, using my weight to push him off-balance. He hissed and skidded back, tail lashing, regaining control by flaring his wings.

"Going soft?" he taunted. "Or is it your human mate slowing you down?"

That was it. I would kill the *kervash*.

I lunged, swords blazing in twin arcs. He ducked under the first, but the second sliced a shallow line across his shoulder. He jerked away, blinking surprise. A scowl contorted his features, but he hid it quickly. The crowd rumbled with excitement, boots and claws drumming on stone.

His next barrage came in a whirlwind of steel. I locked one sword with his dagger and blocked the second with the flat of my other blade, but he drove his knee into my abdomen. Air whooshed from my lungs, and I staggered. My tail whipped to keep me upright, but he was already repositioning for another strike at my head. Instinct roared through me. I raised a sword in desperation—he deflected it but lost his angle, forcing him to sidestep instead of landing the killing blow.

I reeled back, gritting my teeth. Blood dripped down my side; the earlier cut on my arm stung every time I shifted. But I saw a flicker of irritation in his eyes—he'd wanted me down by now.

He laughed, breathless. "You're persistent, I'll give you that."

I answered by rushing forward. My left blade clashed with his right dagger, and I slammed my shoulder into him, with raw force instead of grace. He stumbled, trying to bring up his second blade, but I spun, driving my tail into his ribs. A wet crack echoed. He coughed in pain and hopped back, favoring his side. My pulse hammered, every muscle shaking with the effort to keep going.

Zarvash tried to mask his grimace with a sneer. His chest rose and fell fast.

I advanced methodically, swords at the ready. He bared his teeth and lunged. Our weapons clashed in a frenzy, metal shrieking. His tail lashed for my legs, and I leaped aside at the last moment, bringing both swords down in a punishing overhead strike. He crossed his daggers to block, but the raw heat from my blades caused him to yelp. The impact forced him to his knees for a moment. He managed to roll clear, panting.

I glanced at Orla again, saw her lips parted, her fists clenched. She might've been bruised and burned, but her spirit flared bright as ever. I inhaled, felt the burn in the air coil in my lungs, and charged Zarvash before he could regain footing.

This time, I anticipated his tail strike and smashed it aside with the flat of one blade. He tried to slash at me with a dagger, but I slammed my other sword against his wrist, twisting it free of the weapon. His blade clattered away. He hissed in pain, eyes wild. He had only one dagger left.

He tried to pivot, but I drove my knee into his wounded shoulder, followed by a vicious elbow to his jaw. He crumpled with a snarl. I pressed the tip of a sword to his throat, chest heaving. The crowd drew closer, hunger on every face. The air smelled of sweat and scorched metal.

"Yield," I snarled.

He glared, blood trickling from his lip. For an instant, I thought he might grab for his lost dagger and keep fighting out of spite. Then a flicker of fear crossed his face. His hands rose, empty. "I yield."

The crowd erupted. I stepped back, my swords still at the ready, but the fight was over. Zarvash had lost, and he knew it. Anything but abject surrender now would mean certain death.

Pyroth stepped in, arms raised to quell any objections. "The duel is finished," he announced, voice echoing along the carved ceiling. "By the old ways, Rath Flame Heart stands victorious."

The small crowd erupted again, their cheers and jeers blending into a deafening riot of noise. I ignored them, my focus shifting to Orla. She stood at the edge of the onlookers, her eyes locked on me, her face pale but determined. Selene was beside her, the medkit still in hand, but Orla's attention was entirely on me. She gave me a small nod, her lips curving into a faint smile, and I felt a surge of pride.

She was alive. She was safe. And she was mine.

Zarvash climbed to his feet, his movements stiff and deliberate. His eyes burned with hatred as he glared at me, but he didn't speak.

Pyroth inclined his head. "Honor the terms of your defeat, Zarvash. You will be bound to Rath's judgement for a year's cycle. If you break the vow, you risk exile—or worse."

Zarvash spat on the stone near my feet but didn't speak. He shoved past the ring of Drakarn, ignoring their jeers, and vanished down a side passage.

Heat pounded in my veins, adrenaline slow to fade. I looked to Orla. She limped forward, leaning on Selene, but her eyes were locked on me. Relief battled with lingering fury on her face.

"You did it," she said, voice tight. "Idiot."

"Is that my mating name?" I slid my swords into their sheaths, fighting the urge to collapse from sheer exhaustion.

Selene cleared her throat, rummaging in her medkit. "Can we tend to you both now, or do you plan on fighting for who keels over first?"

Orla grimaced at that. I gently placed a hand against her shoulder, guiding her toward the bench. "We'll let you do your job," I told Selene.

Orla squeezed my arm. "That was reckless," she muttered, but a hint of pride colored her voice. "I'm glad you won."

I gave her a short nod, not trusting myself to speak. The red haze of my anger still vibrated under my skin. We were alive, together. That had to be enough.

Pyroth approached. "You fought well, Flame Heart," he said, his voice low and respectful. "The Forge has judged you worthy."

I nodded, my chest still heaving from the fight. "And Zarvash?"

Pyroth's lips curled into a faint smile. "He is bound to you now. For a year, he will serve you, as is tradition."

I didn't need Zarvash's service. What I needed was his absence. But I didn't say it. The rules of a traditional duel were complex. Zarvash was not my servant, but he would owe me. It was something I would keep in mind in the coming months.

I had a feeling I would need to.

Pyroth left us, and Orla shuddered. I caught her but stumbled and had to shift my stance to right myself.

"You both need the healing caverns," Selene said. "Now."

This time, neither me nor my mate argued.

NINETEEN
ORLA

I leaned over the low table, sketching rough lines across my notebook while my tongue caught on the inside of my cheek. My notes were all around me, half-chaotic, held together by a tenuous thread of logic I might lose if I didn't finish this diagram tonight.

Across from me, Rath sprawled lazily on the bed, one wing draped off the side and a faint smirk tugging at his mouth. His brooding had melted away, replaced instead with the kind of loose relaxation that made him dangerous. His focus shifted between his claw—idly balancing one of my pens—and me, his golden eyes glinting with some private amusement.

You would never guess that two weeks ago we'd

been limping out the Mating Challenge, skin burned and scales bleeding. My ankle would be scarred forever, but thanks to Selene's mending and some Volcarian healing herbs, we were both almost as good as new.

"You're scowling again," he said, his voice like gravel warming under flame. "I almost pity whatever you're planning to conquer."

I didn't look up from the page, instead using the edge of my graphite to shade another section of the proposed geothermal grid system. "I told you, this isn't for war. It's energy distribution."

"Which is also conquest," he drawled, flipping the pen in a slow arc. It clattered to the floor when his claws misjudged the catch, but he didn't bother retrieving it, his gaze homing in on me now. "Sweeter when your enemy is tradition, no?"

I snorted, finally meeting his eyes. "Tradition as an enemy? I'm sure that would make any Blade Councilor faint just hearing it."

"Not me." His tail flicked once, the spaded end curling around the chaise's base. "But I'm less faint-prone than most. Go on, tell me how this marvel of yours will upend generations."

I leaned back, pushing away the hair that always fell into my face when I was working and leaving a faint, unintentional charcoal streak down my temple. "Right now, Scalvaris relies too heavily on heat crystals and lavaforges. They're inefficient for consistent power. The underground geothermal vents could provide scalable energy storage—enough to keep the city's entire infrastructure running without burning through resources." I jabbed the pencil against the edge of the diagram in emphasis. "It's basic science."

"Basic for you," he corrected, his smile deepening. "Try explaining 'scalable energy storage' to Nyktral from the River's Teeth. I think I saw him lick a rock once just because it was shiny."

Laughing, I tossed my pencil onto the table and stretched my arms, sore from hours of scribbling. "You're not wrong. I doubt they'd listen to anything I said even if I dumbed it down. Humans are still aliens. Outsiders."

His expression flickered, something darker passing over his features before he banished it. "Humans may be new arrivals," he said, voice low, "but ideas are not species-bound."

"It's not the ideas they'll fight—it's me having them." I exhaled, frustration churning my thoughts. "I'm still hearing whispers about whether I 'earned' my place."

Rath shifted forward, leaning his elbows onto his

knees until his massive frame made my cramped work area feel even smaller. The hearthlight carved shadows into the planes of his face, highlighting scars I was still learning to trace with my fingertips. "They won't dare call me weak. Not to my face," he said, and though his voice was calm, there was steel hidden beneath the embers. "And they won't call you less than worthy once I've reminded them how valuable you are."

I was getting used to the possessiveness in his tone—it still caught me slightly off guard. Another part of me, the part that had already learned how unwavering he was in his loyalty, found comfort in it. He didn't consider me a weakness; he called me his equal, his strength. And yet ...

"I don't want this to be about you having to defend me. Again," I said, curling my fingers against the edge of the notebook. "I want them to respect me on my own terms."

Rath tilted his head. His amusement returned in a flash. "Foolish mate," he murmured, something softer threading through the words. "You think tearing down centuries of rigid thought happens in a single strike? Lay the foundation for now. I'll keep the others too occupied to sabotage it."

The sudden, delighted laugh that bubbled out of

me startled us both. "So your plan is to just distract Scalvaris while I sneakily modernize it?"

"Exactly." He leaned back again. "Swords clash loudly, *shyrarva*, but it's the quiet forge that alters their edges."

I shook my head, fighting a smile as I returned to my diagram. "God, you're impossible," I muttered, but there was no heat in it.

"And you're brilliant." His rumble chased warmth up my spine, his voice wrapping around my resolve and bolstering it in a way no plan or blueprint could.

His tail coiled and uncoiled lazily as he watched me return to my work. His presence was a strange paradox—calming in its weight, but always charged with the potential for motion, for violence, for some deep and electric possibility. I'd seen him fight, seen the beast in him unleashed, but there, in the privacy of our chambers, he was something entirely different.

When the hiss of his shifting weight broke the quiet, I glanced up to see him rising from the bed with his usual predatory grace. His wings flexed once in a low sweep before folding close to his back, sharp edges catching the firelight. He crossed the room, his broad size shrinking even our spacious quarters, and began rummaging in one of the storage compartments carved into the volcanic rock walls.

"What are you doing?" I asked.

He didn't answer, at least not vocally. His tail flicked in what I'd come to recognize as either amusement or mischief—possibly both—before he pulled something from the compartment and hid it behind his back.

"Rath," I said, skeptical. His eyes caught mine, a slight glint of smugness visible in their depths. "What are you hiding?"

Instead of answering, he crossed back to me, his movements deliberate, and crouched just close enough for his heat to bleed into my space. The sharp planes of his features softened slightly as he tilted his head, studying me, something achingly gentle shimmering just beneath the habitual intensity of his gaze.

"Close your notebook," he murmured.

I blinked, thrown off by the sudden and quietly commanding tone. Then I folded the paper closed, placing it to the side without comment. "Alright," I said slowly. "What's—"

His hand came forward, producing a roll of parchment with a flourish. The edges were worn—coated with soot and age, its once-dark ink faded to a muted charcoal. He placed it carefully in front of me, sliding it closer before stepping back to observe my reaction.

Curious, I gently unfurled the scroll. My lips parted as the full scope of it came into view: a star chart, impossibly intricate, the precise marks of constellations spiraling outward from a central axis. I wasn't just looking at a map of Volcaryth's night skies —it cataloged movements and highlighted solar alignments with precision that should've been impossible for such an old artifact.

"This," I breathed, running my finger just shy of touching the delicate ink. "This is incredible, Rath. How ... how did you find this?"

"The archives beneath the Blade Keep," he replied, his voice quieter than usual yet brimming with hidden significance. "Forgotten, abandoned in storage with documents no one cares about anymore —old star maps from times long gone."

I swallowed hard, the enormity of it sinking in. "Why now? Why ... why show me this?"

He didn't hesitate. "Because I know your mind, Orla. Your eyes always watch fractured things—the cracks between stone, the marrow in what others throw away. You follow patterns no one else sees." He crouched again, heavy gaze pinning me in place.

"You'll see more in this map than anyone else has for centuries. And I wonder what you might uncover."

His words struck something within me, leaving me disarmed. I looked back at the star map, tracing its curves. Part of me wanted to devour it with analysis, to pull its meanings apart and piece them back into a constellation of discovery.

"It's beautiful," I said finally, my voice catching against the lump in my throat. My gaze darted upward. "You're full of surprises."

His lips tugged into a faint smirk, but his tail's restless flick betrayed his satisfaction. "Only for you," he said, his voice dipping into that dangerous warmth that had undone pieces of me before.

I couldn't suppress the smile spreading across my lips as I carefully rolled the star chart back into its delicate form, gripping it tighter than I needed to. It was more than ancient parchment filled with forgotten starlore—it was trust, belief, and an unspoken promise etched in the gesture of giving it to me.

"Rath," I whispered, unable to find words fitting enough for gratitude or depth. Instead, when I lifted my gaze to him again, every unsaid thing burned in the glance we exchanged, a gravity like twin suns aligning.

His hand reached out, the claws soft as they skimmed along my jawline. His wings arched outward slightly, the tension there not from threat but something raw. "I wanted you to have something worthy of your vision," he rumbled, thumb brushing along the hollow of my cheekbone. "And let it remind you, I see in you what others cannot."

My heart was thundering. Not from fear, though the intensity in Rath's gaze could incinerate lesser nerves—but from the overwhelming sense of being known. Of being seen.

I swallowed hard, my tongue darting out to wet my lips. His thumb stilled on my cheek, the motion not lost on him. Of course it wasn't. When I finally managed to speak, my voice emerged softer than I had intended. "You ... you do that a lot, you know."

His head tilted just slightly, his pupils narrowing in curiosity. "Do what?"

"See me." My hand strayed upward, resting lightly on his forearm. "Really see me."

His scrutiny deepened. "Because you are worth seeing, *shyrarva*," he said, his voice dropping into something dangerously tender. "Worth everything."

The air between us shifted, like the faint rattle just before a storm unleashes itself. My breath hitched, but there was no holding back the words now scrambling over one another to escape my throat.

"I love you." The admission sounded almost foreign, like it had been sitting just under the surface of my skin, waiting for this precise moment to escape.

Rath froze. Not in shock. It was something quieter, something deeper. A pause as though the very world had stopped to allow his next breath to find its way into his chest. The tension in his jaw eased first, then his wings, which curled protectively inward as he leaned ever so slightly closer.

"Say it again," he growled, low and rough, his tone making the space between my ribs tremble.

A strange, soft laugh bubbled out of me, more exhale than sound. "I love you," I repeated, each word deliberately climbing its way through whatever walls still existed between us. And now that I'd said it, I found I wanted to say it forever.

His broad frame stretched taller, his shoulders loosening like some invisible weight had finally lifted. He sank to his knees in front of me, tilting me forward as his hands—which could shatter steel but touched me like glass—came to rest on either side of my hips.

Rath's gaze burned, the liquid fire of his pupils

expanding, engulfing every hesitance in their way. "And I—" His voice faltered, cracked like rock encountering a river, and he paused before adjusting with deliberate clarity, quieter now, but no less powerful for it. "And I love you, *shyrarva*. More than you understand."

There it was. Plain, simple—except none of it was simple. It existed like an avalanche, unstoppable now that it had begun. My chest felt both weightless and bursting, filled by the thunder of his truth clasping itself to mine.

I smiled. "There's not much I don't understand."

His answering grin was slow. "Good," he murmured, his lips brushing my temple as he rose to tower over me, never letting his hands stray farther than my frame.

His lips lingered at my temple, the warmth of his breath sweeping over my skin. My eyes drifted shut as every sharp-edged worry fell away, replaced by a sense of boundless heat and safety. His hands, one resting on my hip and the other at the curve of my lower back, tightened almost imperceptibly, their claws careful crescents against my body.

"*Shyrarva*," he murmured, pulling back just enough to match my gaze. His voice was a fire-fed growl, but there was no urgency in it this time—just depth and need. "Will you let me show you?"

"Show me what?" The question barely left me, not because I doubted, but because his intensity rendered words almost secondary.

His tail coiled gently around my ankle, claiming the space between us as his claws flexed slightly. "What it means to be mine."

Heat flared in my chest, his unsaid promise an all consuming weight. I couldn't have defied that pull if I tried—and stars above, I didn't want to try. My fingers lightly traced the ridges along his forearm as I nodded, my pulse loud enough in my ears to drown out everything else.

"Always."

Rath held me carefully, my ribs pressing against the solid weight of his chest as his wings arched slightly. For a creature designed to bring a battlefield to its knees, he carried me like I might shatter if he held on too hard.

He stepped backward until his claws grazed the edge of the raised sleeping slab in the center of the room, its surface draped in silks.

Rath laid me down, one hand bracing the line of my spine while the other adjusted my shoulders into place until the silks cradled my weight. His wings spread fully for balance before he joined me, the rumble in his chest steady as the earth itself.

"You are ..." His voice hitched, his golden eyes awash with something both worshipful and predatory as his claws curled around one of my thighs. "You are fire itself, *shyrarva*, and you do not know."

"You keep calling me fire," I murmured, my hands sliding up his shoulders until they curled around his neck, fingers grazing the seam where muscle and scale met. "What does that make you?"

"Fuel," he answered, his fangs catching on the word like a vow. "Heat without direction will devour everything it touches. But with purpose?" His tongue flicked along his fangs, his tail brushing over my calf in slow, deliberate arcs. "It sustains, binds, creates."

His mouth captured mine before the quiver in my breath could answer him, his kiss measured and slow at first, then hungrier when I pressed up into him. His claws skimmed just under the hem of my shirt, tracing the faint lines of muscle where the burn scars were beginning to fade.

He broke away just long enough for his fingers to tug delicately at the fabric. "Off," he commanded, his gaze nearly black. His claws rested against the edge of my skin. "Let me see everything."

My clothes joined the folds of silk beneath me, but his lips didn't follow immediately.

Instead, his fingers skimmed over my exposed skin, tracing over burns, scars, and the star tattoos he'd come to know better than I did. His tail looped farther across my legs, pinning me gently in place as his claws caught at the line of my ribs. "They'll know," he murmured, lips finding the hollow just beneath my collarbone. "Every mark etched here is proof of a strength they can never question. Never challenge."

I would have laughed if his thumb hadn't caught on the corner of my hip bone, stopping the sound with a sharp inhale. "You think scars impress them more than schematics?"

"I know," he said simply, his lips skimming lower, tongue brushing just shy of the lines between silk and skin. Every nerve in my body sang under his touch.

"Rath, I—" The words stumbled into the space between us, more reflexive gasp than command as his mouth found the edge of mine again.

Fingertips against my hip flexed, claws hidden away for just the barest press of intention—Rath's reverence was fire made flesh, devouring without destruction. And when his tail dragged higher, the heat at its core left no confusion: He wasn't asking if I understood.

He was showing me.

Claiming me.

Loving me.

I arched into him, the heat from my own need melding with the furnace of his scales as his claws dipped in places that made me shiver. His hips pressed flush with mine as his tail curled tighter—a possessive pressure rather than restraint, his voice lurching into a quiet growl.

Mine.

The word echoed silently as he consumed me, entirely his own.

Shyrarva.

His breath drew short against my ear, claws flexing protectively across my ribs, but his thrusts slowed with effort. His rhythm stuttered before settling—he intended it to, his movements deliberate and languid. No hurry here, not when it was just us.

Just this undeniable pull.

"Rath," I gasped, my hands clawing at him as he brought me to the edge, forcing me to hover there.

He shuddered, his lips at my neck as his pace faltered. "Burn for me, *shyrarva.*"

He didn't have to ask. The sensation he wrung

from me was already fire itself, but his command set something loose that raged and devoured until there was nothing left.

He joined me in an all-consuming wave, his chest pressed flush to mine, his wings folded tightly over both of us. His breaths came deep and hard, the satisfaction in them unmistakable. When he finally spoke, his voice was a low rumble.

"Never forget who you are," he murmured, his fangs glinting even as his grip softened.

I turned my face against his neck, breathing in the scent of him—charred cedar and embers—as I smiled into his skin. "You can remind them every time I forget."

EPILOGUE

Vyne

The market buzzed—too loud, too alive. I hovered at the edge of the chaos, half-draped in shadows. The crystals in the walls seemed to burn, casting fractured light over the crowd. It made their faces sharp, jagged, almost unreal.

Yet her face, among the other humans, stuck out like a spark waiting to catch.

A burst of laughter, human and soft, carried over rattling carts and shouted negotiations. The sound hit me like a foreign blade, unfamiliar and fatally precise. My tongue ached, that strange sensitivity crawling up from the back of my throat and settling deep in my chest.

For days ... longer than days, if I was being honest, I'd tried to ignore it.

I wouldn't be Rath, drawn in like a moth to fire despite knowing how it would scorch. I was sharper than that. My sense of self-preservation still had teeth.

But when she laughed again, my body betrayed me, dragging my gaze toward their group. Four of them together, a tight-knit cluster navigating the crowd with cautious joy. They moved like a flock of sunglow finches, all darting movements and quiet giggles bound by instinctive camaraderie. They were softer than anything else in the market. Their fragility was jarring, delicate within the sharp angles of Scalvaris.

Delicate, but not weak.

Her hair caught my attention first. Light caught the strands as she tilted her head toward another of the women, listening intently to their whispered conversation. A smirk tugged at the corner of her lips. A quiet predator, watching and observing before striking with some dry quip, I wagered.

It wasn't her beauty, though she had enough of it to snap a weaker male's resolve. It wasn't the way she tucked her hands close to her chest when the smallest Drakarn child ran past her clutching sticky scales of stolen candy. And it damn well wasn't the slight upward curve of her jawline showing off the tension in her neck as her smirk relaxed back into something unreadable.

It was her scent—a phantom warmth that lingered on the smoke-filled air. Something sweet, slightly sharp underneath, like phoenix fruit steeped in herb oil. The scent tightened every nerve in my body, something wild yanking at my restraint.

My tongue tingled again, sharper this time, as if some unseen force had lashed it. It made me want to step forward, part the crowd surrounding them, and inhale until my chest finally stopped burning.

I retreated deeper into the shadows, claws twitching uselessly at my sides. What was this, exactly? Was it the same tethering madness that had dragged Rath through the hells for his human? That had made Darrokar act like a fool?

I clenched my jaws, the barbell in my tongue clicking against my teeth. Whatever it was, it needed to stop.

Rath had barely survived the upheaval caused by his bond. He'd fought tooth and claw against Karyseth and the vultures circling Scalvaris's politics.

I didn't have his patience or his recklessness. I'd

spent most of my life artfully dancing just under the council's scrutiny, dodging unnecessary risks and skulking out of the spotlight.

Her laughter cut through me again, raw as an open wound. It scraped away the pretense I clung to, the false calm I'd worn like armor for so long.

I was supposed to be good at ignoring stupid ideas. At looking through the fire and thinking about my next move. But suddenly, I was back at the edges of the market without realizing my feet had moved. The women were still there, farther ahead now, lingering near a vendor draped with polished obsidian necklaces. She stood apart from her companions, fingers pressed to a lichen-brushed gemstone, her expression thoughtful.

The ache twisted tighter. My tail jerked in protest, smacking a low crate behind me with a crack, forcing me to snap it, controlled again.

"Fucking idiot," I hissed under my breath.

To her, from a distance, I probably looked no better than some hulking stalker with half a brain.

But she didn't notice me. No one did—not even the vendor, who was preoccupied arguing with another Drakarn over the price of lava-lizard talons decorated in intricate painted patterns. It was easy to slip closer. Close enough to see the faint drag marks in the dust where her boots had scuffed the ground. Close enough to think about reaching out ... for what, I didn't even know.

The scent hit me harder now. Impossible not to notice when it wrapped around me like a second skin, pulling me in like the currents of an underground river. My tongue burned red hot, every sensitive tastebud lighting up with phantom flavor.

It would be so easy to close the distance. To press clawed fingers lightly to her shoulder so she'd turn. To watch as her wide, unfamiliar human eyes took me in. To speak—just one word, a name, her name. Or to say nothing at all and just let the silence stretch between us, burning this unnatural pull into the fabric of what could become ...

Would become nothing.

I dragged the thought back, sharp as my blades. Nothing. No "could," no "would."

A mate—a *human*—wasn't something I could claim. Not now, not ever. Karyseth's schemes against Rath and Orla proved that truth well enough.

Why would I want to give her another opening? Rath and Orla had already survived enough. I wasn't about to play with lava after their fragile truce.

Something in me hardened as I stepped away

again, the ache in my chest twisting into something closer to a wound.

Self-inflicted. Necessary.

I turned, setting my path deliberately away from the market's packed heart. "Be smarter than him, you idiot," I muttered to the emptiness ahead. I repeated it like a mantra, the words as bitter as sand trapped under my tongue.

Be smarter than Rath. Be smarter.

But even as I turned my back on her, I swore I could still taste the way her scent lingered on the grit-flavored air.

And the burn wouldn't subside.

What's next in this series:
Scorched by Fate
Find out more

Thank you so much for reading *Echoes of Fire*!

Your support means the world to me. If you enjoyed the story, it would mean even more if you could take a moment to share your thoughts in a review or leave a rating.

Hearing from readers like you makes all the difference!

Need a little more of Rath & Orla?

Sign up at the link below to **receive a free bonus epilogue!**

Get your freebie!
https://katerudolph.net/index.php/rath-bonus/

WHAT TO READ NEXT: SCORCHED
BY FATE

I am a Drakarn forgemaster, sculptor of steel, master of fire. My world is heat and metal. I control the flame, bend it to my will.

But her? She is wildfire. And I am losing control.

Selene is flame wrapped in human skin—fierce, unyielding, utterly captivating. She speaks in sharp words and soft touches, a warrior and healer who sets my blood ablaze.

Her presence consumes me. Her scent lingers in my lungs, her ferocity fuels my hunger.

To the depths of my soul, I know she is my mate.

But I cannot claim her. She is off-limits.

Untouchable.

Yet when a deadly sickness strikes Scalvaris and the only cure lies deep in the treacherous Harrovan

Mountains, I am the one who must go with her. The one who must keep her safe.

The pull between us is undeniable. Every glance, every breath, a battle I am losing.

She is determined to find the cure. I am determined to resist her.

But when the mountains test us, when fire and danger close in, I will show her the truth written in my soul...

She belongs to me.

EXILE'S HUNTER
ALIEN MATES: PLANET EXILE
KATE RUDOLPH

Exile's Hunter

Kenzie will do anything to save her sister... even if it means teaming up with a dangerous alien who makes her heart pound.

Kenzie has crossed the galaxy in search of her abducted sister and she's finally landed on Guerran. It's a planet full of criminals and she can trust no one, especially not the terrifyingly hot alien named Mad.

He's as much a criminal as anyone on Guerran. And he's her only hope. But she isn't sure whether she should kiss him or stab him when his presence makes her heat up with desire.

Mad can't leave the exile planet. Once Kenzie finds Carise, the sisters will be long gone. There's no future between her and the hunky alien, no matter how quickly he steals her heart.

How can Kenzie walk away when fate has put her in the path of her mate?

Exile's Adored

Help isn't coming.

When Carise wakes up on an alien planet running is her only chance at escape, even if being caught means death.

She'd rather die than face whatever her captors plan to do to her.

Guerran is no safe place for healing and every moment is fear. Until Jaek, a gentle giant of an alien, makes himself her protector. But when their fragile bond is tested, Carise knows she must find strength within herself to become brave enough to survive Guerran.

This time she won't let herself be taken. And she's not leaving her mate behind.

Dragon Brides
Dragon Princes. Fierce Women. Love.
Fated mates, fierce women, and dragon princes are
ready to find their mates.

Crux

Ranger

Saber

Cipher

Storm

Drake

Asher

Knox

Flint

Pine

Guarded by the Shifter

Werewolf. Bodyguard. Mate.
The origins of these shifters are shrouded in mystery, but they're determined to protect their mates from any harm that comes their way.
Also available in audio!
Hunting Season
On the Prowl
Stalking Magic
Hungry for the Wolf
Wolf Cursed (novella)
Wolf's Temptation

Stealing the Alpha

The thief takes what she wants, but the alpha keeps what's his...
Join shifter thief Mel as she clashes with lion alpha Luke in an explosive trilogy of two opposites who can't keep away from one another.
Also available in audio!

The Alpha Heist
Entangled with the Thief
In the Alpha's Bed

Alien Mates: Planet Exile

Guerran is no place for pretty human women. But these alien heroes will protect their mates!
Also available in audio!

Exile's Hunter
Exile's Adored

Zulir Warrior Mates

Kidnapped humans. Alien Warriors. Electric wings.
The Zulir Warrior Mates series brings you human heroines and heroes abducted from Earth who find love – and wings! – with the alien warriors who rescue them.
Also available in audio!

Synnr's Saint
Synnr's Hope
Synnr's Spark
Synnr's Kiss
Synnr's Ride

Mated to the Alien

Fated Mate Alien Romance

Detyens are doomed to die young if they don't find their fated mates.

Follow along as these mated pairs fight off aliens, corrupt dictators, prejudiced humans, pirates, and more! The books can be read or listened to in any order, though some characters show up in multiple stories.

Select books available in audio.

Pick a book and jump into the action today!

Ruwen

Tyral

Stoan

Cyborg

Krayter

Kayleb

Shayn

Braxtyn

Doryan

Dekon

Detyen Warriors

Detya was destroyed a hundred years ago. These doomed warriors are out to find justice… and their mates.
The Detyen Warriors series brings you kick butt heroines, alpha alien heroes, fated mates, and relationships strong enough to span the galaxy!
The entire series is also available in audio!

Soulless

Ruthless

Heartless

Faultless

Endless

Detyen Warrior Outcasts

Fated Mate Alien Romance

These doomed warriors were abandoned by their people and live on the edge. Their mates hold the key to their salvation.
Pick a book and jump into the action today!

Dangerous Bond
Intrepid Bond
Wayward Bond

Alien Holiday Romance

Christmas… in space????
These alien holiday romances look beyond Earth's winter holidays and ring in the season across the galaxy!
Select titles available in audio.
Snowed in with the Alien Beast
The Alien's Winter Gift
The Alien Reindeer's Wild Ride
Trapped with her Alien Mate

Alien Outlaws

Outlaws, schemes, and love… it's all there in the Alien Outlaws series…

Andie Munster is sick of life on Ixilta, the planet she got dumped on after being abducted from Earth six years ago. And when the mysterious and dangerous Xandr shows up looking for a way off the planet, she's half-prisoner, half-co-conspirator in a wild rush to escape.

Rogue Alien's Escape
Rogue Alien's Woman
Rogue Alien's Secret
Rogue Alien's Legacy

Find more by Kate Rudolph at www. katerudolph.net

ABOUT KATE RUDOLPH

Kate Rudolph is a paranormal and sci-fi romance writer who lives in Indiana. She loves writing about kick butt heroines and the steamy heroes who love them. She's been devouring romance novels since she was too young to be reading them and had to hide her books so no one would take them away. She couldn't imagine a better job in this world than writing romances and sharing them with her fellow readers.

If you enjoyed this story, please consider leaving a review.

www.ingramcontent.com/pod-product-compliance
Lightning Source LLC
Chambersburg PA
CBHW060908210726
48293CB00006B/2011